Achilles Heel

Nefetiri Frazier

DEDICATION

David Frazier

CONTENTS

ACKNOWLEDGMENTS

KDP

Chapter One

Samora

As I walked through the courtyard, on my way to the art building, I couldn't help but notice Ares Turner leaning against the trunk of the oak tree with his eyes glued to his phone. That day he was wearing a black leather jacket with a grey V-neck and some shredded skinny jeans. His black hair was shorter than it was before. He'd missed some school because his mother passed away. I tripped over my own feet from staring too hard, landing right on my stomach. He rushed over and helped me to my feet.

"Are you alright?" He looked me over with concern.

I adjusted my bag strap. "Yes...I'm fine." I dusted the dirt and blades of grass from my skirt.

We both had ceramics class for first period, and he took his seat next to me. He truly had a talent that exceeded beyond anyone in our class. The art piece that he'd been working on before he left was a woman with a hole in her chest and her broken heart perched on her lap. He applied so much detail into her work. she was very realistic. I could only assume that it was his mother.

After Mr. Gold took attendance, I made my way over to my locker and retrieved my mermaids. I was in the process of sanding her at the time. I dropped her off at my desk and was heading back to my locker to get the sanding paper when I heard something shatter to pieces. Everyone gathered around the kiln room.

Ares was on his knees with the severed head of his masterpiece in his hands. The remnants were scattered about the floor. His teeth were clenched as he threw the head on the floor. It shattered into a million tiny pieces like the rest of his work. He sprang to his feet "You are freaking prick!" Ares gave Erik a good punch to the face. Blood began to travel down his busted lip. Hellfire was blazing behind Erik's brown eyes as he knocked Ares to the ground, and they began to tussle. Mr. Gold surged through the crowd and broke up the fight.

Erik and Ares were once friends, but a girl tore them apart.

The girl was named Megan and she moved away

Erik was envious of Ares because she chose him. You would have thought that he would have cut Ares some slack after the guy got back from burying his mother. I was so outraged that when Mr. Gold Marched them both to the principal's office, I swept up the broken pieces. It saddened me to think that after all of his hard work he would have to start from scratch.

Mr. Gold eventually returned to class and found me dumping the remains into the trashcan.

"Oh, you didn't have to clean that up."

"It was no big deal." I placed the broom back in the corner of the room with the dustpan attached.

"Since you were so helpful to me today, I will give you an extra day to finish sanding your mermaid."

" It's okay. I can come in at lunch."

"Are you sure?" He stepped aside as I exited the kiln room.

"I'm sure." That day my best friend Arianna was out with a cold and I really missed my friend, and I didn't want to spend my lunch break eating alone. That afternoon she would be in for a huge surprise when I filled her in about today's unfortunate events.

When lunchtime rolled in, I grabbed a salad and water from the cafeteria. I normally brought my lunch, but I was in a rush to get to school that morning. On my way out, someone captured me by the arm. I spun around and gasped.

"I heard that you cleaned up my mess." He rubbed the back of his neck with an awkward expression.

"It was the least I could do. You have been slaving away on it so long that you shouldn't have had to clean it up."

His eyes widened. " Thanks for being considerate of my feelings. I honestly didn't think anyone cared."

My cheeks were on the brink of combustion. "No problem."

"Are you going back to the art room?"

"Yes. I didn't get much sanding done."

"We can go together. I have a ton of work to do myself."

With that being said, we walked in together. Once I had my mermaid on my desk and started sanding it down, the sound of his kneading the clay and slamming it down on the desk echoed through the air. His nostrils were flaring, and his eyes were watering. I could tell that he was not only using this as an opportunity to catch up but as a much-needed therapy session. My heart truly went out to him that day.

After school was out and my homework was complete, I logged into my email account and was shocked to see a friend request from Ares. He never even popped up as a friend suggestion. I hit accept and instantly his chat head popped up. My heart was pounding like crazy as those three dots, indicating that he was typing, flashed on the screen.

Ares: I just wanted to say thanks again for being supportive. I hope that I didn't scare you off at lunch today. I really needed to channel my frustration into my work. I'm not crazy. I promise.

Samora: I don't think you gave off that vibe. You have been through a lot and you need to unleash those emotions somehow. I'm sorry. I forgot to thank you for helping me up from the ground this morning.

Ares: It was no problem. Would you like to join me in the art room tomorrow? It feels nice having someone else around.

Samora: Sure. It's time for me to glaze my mermaid anyway.

Ares: See you then.

Samora: alright. Have a good night.

After getting off the computer with him, I called up Arianna and filled her in.

"Oh, my gosh! Is the end of the world coming tomorrow? I think you just landed yourself a boyfriend."

My cheeks were blazing. "You know that my dad won't let me go off with just anyone. Besides, I think he's just being nice. Today is the first time that we spoke to each other."

"Man, I can't wait to get back to school. You haven't dated anyone since last year. This would be good for the both of you."

"You weren't listening to a single thing I said." I rolled my eyes and called it a night

Chapter Two

Samora

When I set foot on campus, I was instantly blinded by a familiar pair of feminine hands that were lavender scented. I could hear the sound of her metal bracelets clank together.

" Guess who?"

"Arianna, you are the only girl I hang out with at this school."

She removed her hands from my face and linked arms with me. "What are you talking about? I'm the only one that you hang out with."

"That is true." I laughed.

We made our way over to the D building where the vending machine was. Arianna and I never went a morning without getting ourselves a coffee energy drink and some pastries. That morning I went for the apple pastry.

We took our usual spot on the Bench beneath the rows and rows of yearbook photos of the students from the previous years. I removed the plastic from my pastry and tossed it in the trashcan nearby.

"So, where is your dark prince at?"

"Don't call him that." I cracked open my energy drink and took a sip.

"If he's into you then we should go find him this morning." She stashed what was left of her pastry into her bag and rose from the bench. I wasn't about to waste mine. I munched away.

"Shove that face and let's get going!" She grabbed me by the hand and dragged me off the bench. I was forced to shove the rest of my pastry in my bag.

"Don't you understand how desperate this comes off?" I whined. She spotted him making his way to the art building and called out to him. He turned to see who the voice belonged to and stopped in front of the entrance.

"What up?"

That's what I would like to know.

"I'm sorry about what happened to your art. Erik is such a jerk. I should go and give him a piece of my mind."

"I can handle myself. He must be going through some sort of emotional turmoil to lash out at a grieving person. Thanks anyway."

"You are heading in early to catch up on your work?" I asked.

He snap- pointed at me. " That's right." He held the door open for us.

Once we were inside, Arianna helped me get my materials. I couldn't decide on what glaze to use, so I held up a glaze that turned silver after being baked. Then I held up one that made it turn purple. I didn't want different glazes for each portion of her. Ares walked by and tapped on the silver. I was sold. Arianna gave me a nudge and a wink on the way back to my desk.

As I started to glaze my mermaid, Arianna was looking through her messages when she came across an invite to a party from her cousin Liam.
"Would you guys be up for a party this weekend?"

"I don't know if my dad would let me go." I frowned, coating the mermaids' face with the glaze.

"I'm down. Could I bring someone with me?"

Did he have a girlfriend?

"I'm sure you can. Uhm... who did you have in mind?"

I was glad that she asked for me. Things were awkward enough.

"My friend Joseph."

"Cool. Cool." She handed him her phone. "Put your number in my phone and I will text you the details."
With that being said, he did so without giving it a second thought.

"Hey, I'm sure your dad will let you go if you say that you're sleeping over at my place."

"I can ask." I reached into the front pocket of my purse and pulled out my phone. I asked him, hoping that he would say yes. This would provide the perfect chance to get to know Ares better.

Dad: Just be sure to set an alarm.

I was surprised that he agreed without hesitation or inquiring about more information. This would be the first time since the incident that he let me go anywhere. I guess my good behavior was going to be awarded.

"He gave me the okay." Arianna flung her arms around my neck, excitedly.

"This is going to be awesome!" She practically sang.

During lunch, Ares and I walked over to the art building after grabbing lunch. Suddenly Erik popped up. "You hear about that wicked party that's happening tonight?"

"What do you want?" I frowned, holding the door open for Ares and letting the door almost slam in Erik's face.

"I heard that a certain someone is going to be there." He nudged Ares in the arm after catching back up to us.

"Who?" Ares asked in an uninterested tone of voice.

"You know exactly who I'm talking about." Ares slammed the door to his locker, looking ghostly pale.

"When did she get back?"

My eyes began to water as I approached the kiln room. I should have known that there would only be a friendship between us. It was obvious that he still had deep feelings for her. I found my silver mermaid on the rack and took it over to Mr. Gold who was in the middle of grading quizzes.

"I think you did a lovely job." He examined it carefully. "I give it a hundred percent."

That was always good to hear. I was only taking ceramics one and that was the class that didn't require the pottery wheel. At the beginning of the year, we started with coil pots and we were now finishing up the school year experimenting with pottery sculptures.

After school, I ransacked my closet for something to knock everyone's socks off. Especially, if I was going to be fighting for Ares's attention. I found a blue dress that had frilly sleeves and a lace back. It stopped just above the knee and had a split up the side. I shoved it into my bag.

When I was on my way out to the car, my dad hugged me and told me that he wanted me home around twelve the following day.

"I won't forget. See you then." I smiled and tossed my bag into the passenger's seat.

Arianna was in the middle of pouring drinks into red cups that were lined up in rows on the kitchen counter. I raised an eyebrow. " Is the party being held here?"

"Strict parents can be such a damn buzz kill." She sighed.

"Well, that was awfully nice of you to offer your house up for it."

"What can I say?" She shrugged. " I'm a giver."

I got dressed in the downstairs bathroom. When I stepped out, my shoulder-length brown hair was in curls. My almond-shaped eyes were outlined with thin liner. I changed out the nose ring for a small diamond that was star-shaped. I slid into some pumps to match the dress.

When Arianna met me in the hallway, her long, blonde hair was in beach waves. Her green eyes were outlined with silver liner to match her dress and shoes.

The doorbell rang and The first group arrived. They were some college boys. One of them grabbed two drinks and strolled over. He had black hair that was tipped with blue. His eyes were blue, and he had snake piercings. His nose was round, and he had medium lips.

"My name is Ryan. What's yours?" He handed me a cup.

"Samora." I took a drink. I was the kind that needed to show up at the party drunk to be fun. I didn't do well without it.

"Do you go to the university?"

"Back off Ryan. She is only seventeen. "Ryan tossed back some of his drink.

"How do you two know each other?" I asked.

"Believe it or not, but Ryan here grew up next door to me. He even dated my sister for a while. Then she dumped him when she found someone better." Ryan grunted with a wrinkled nose and started chatting up Arianna.

It was refreshing to see him getting back to his old self again.

I lowered my gaze to my drink. " I couldn't help but overhear you talking to Erik earlier about Megan." I tried not to disguise the disappointment in my voice and failing miserably.

He took a drink, as did I. "Apparently she's back in town and going to be here tonight. I thought that she would have told me before Erik." He took another drink and sighed.

"Do you know if she's permanently back?"

He swiveled his cup. I could hear the ice beating against the walls of his cup as he did so. " No, but I don't think things will be the same between us. She kind of left during the worst stages of my grief. The only thing that I will definitely be asking her is, why she left."

I finished off the rest of my drink and excused myself. I told Arianna about the whole thing. She gave me a sympathetic rub on the back. " I knew that you couldn't fool me though. You had been scoping him out for months before the two of you spoke."

"Do you think Juan cursed me?" I took a seat on the arm of the tan sofa next to her.

"Honey, he would have to have a brain to do something like that" I couldn't help but laugh.

When I looked up, the woman of the hour had arrived she was still four foot and skinny. Her red hair flowed all the way down her lower back. Her green eyes scanned the room. It didn't take a rocket scientist to figure out who she was looking for. She was wearing a black blouse, some skinny Jeans
with some flats. When Ares came out of the restroom, he ran right smack into her. Both of them voiced their apologies and then their eyes met, and they shied away from each other. Then they disappeared through the crowd and out the back door.

"Don't you worry! I won't let them sleep together at my party." She clanked her cup to mine and drank some more.

The next person to make his debut was Erik. He came in with a grey V-neck, skinny jeans, and a skull necklace. A girl handed him a drink and whispered something in his ear. The corner of his mouth rose, and his eyes were glued

to her backside as she strolled off. He let out a sigh and
then walked over to us of all people.

"Hey, do you guys know if Ares showed up yet?"

"Yeah. He's outback. With Megan."

" Good." He took a seat on the glass, coffee table in front of
us and took a drink.

"I thought that the two of. you were fighting over Megan."
Came spewing out of my mouth. The booze was kicking in.
My head was feeling a little off.

"I'm so over her. I just want Ares to suffer." He snickered
into the brim of his cup.

" Why are you guys still feuding? He just lost his mother."

His eyes widened with intrigue. "Do you have a thing for
Mr. Dark and brooding?"

"I just think... that you should... be a little nicer to him. I
know that he would cut you some... slack if the roles were
reversed." I hiccupped.

Ares and Megan came back through the glass doors. Ares
spotted us talking with Erik and may have looked confused.

I wasn't sure. His face looked a little blurry. He and Megan walked over. She kindly greeted Arianna and me.

"Erik." She glared. He rolled his eyes and disappeared.

"It has been a while since we last hung out."

"Yeah. The last time that happened you were puking in your mom's expensive bag when we snuck into that nightclub with fakes." Arianna laughed.

"So, what brings you back to this crap town?" I asked.

"I'm visiting my grandma. I will be back in New York by Monday."

Good riddance. I didn't see what the appeal was. Ares was almost six-foot tall. Her eyes were huge and she kind of walked with a hunch. Oh, stop being so mean. You would criticize a unicorn if he were attracted to it and you freaking like unicorns. You pathetic woman!

" What did Erik want?" Area's eyes lingered on mine.

" Nothing." I had to drink some more.

"Is he still stirring up trouble?"

"It's his nature." Arianna laughed.

Megan excused herself for a phone call. There was an awkward silence while we waited for her to return. When she came back, she said that her grandma needed her, and Ares walked her to the door.

"Now that she's out of the way ask him to dance or something?"

"No thanks." My favorite song came on and I was ready for some fun. I walked until I found the center of the bumping and grinding crowd and danced alone, letting the music eliminate all my cares. I finished off my drink and tossed it towards the back wall. It hit Erik in the head, and he started throwing a huge tantrum and grabbed poor Greg Mills by the collar of his shirt and head-butted him.

Arianna came out to join me when a rap song started blasting through the surround speakers that were placed on either side of her parent's fireplace. When the party was over, Ares offered to help us clean up. I was still drunk from it all.

"Thank you. That would be awesome." Arianna slapped a bag and some gloves into his hand.

I sat there on the couch just checking him out. He seemed like he had more muscle tone as he bent over to pick up some red cups to toss them into the bag. When he caught me staring, a smile spread across his face. My heart started pounding violently against my ribs.

"Are you going to help us?" Arianna handed me a broom and dustpan. She dragged me into the kitchen and that was where I got started. There were chips and cupcake crumbs everywhere.

"How do you expect to get a date if you're drooling over him like that?" She shook her head and went over to the sink to scrub some dishes.

"He is just so pretty." I sighed.

She shushed me. "You're hopeless." She laughed. I stuck my tongue out at her. She had me walk him out to the dumpster.

"Did you have fun tonight?"

I gave him a thumbs-up before unlocking the gate. Watching him lift that lid had me biting my bottom lip with my head leaned against the fence. I quickly adjusted my posture when he closed the lid.

I went to sleep that night with a smile on my face.

Chapter Three

Ares

Phase one of my plan was complete. I played the recording that Erik was kind enough to make for me of
the conversation that he had with Samora. She was into me. I hadn't been reading into things. I couldn't help but grin,

remembering how her beautiful body looked out in the crowd. Catching her checking me out was the freaking highlight of my night. She was a walking fantasy for sure. Bringing Megan into this was just a bonus. She was plagued with disappointment when she talked about her. I was going to finish the school year with everything that I wanted. I drummed my hands on the steering wheel to the radio.

I pulled into the parking lot of my apartment. My dad and his girlfriend, Mindy were sitting out on the front balcony, drinking and smoking.

A lot of people said that I took after him, but I couldn't see it. He had beady eyes and a fork nose with paper-thin lips. He had a receding hairline and black, curly locks. His face was rounded off with stubble. He had a potbelly going on.

Mindy on the other hand was physically fit. She was only a sophomore in college. She had a light tan with blonde locks that she clearly dyed. She had plump lips with a mole on the left side of her forehead. She had doe eyes and a butterfly tattoo on her left arm. She was always showing off cleavage.

"Where were you? We needed you to help us move our things into Mindy's

" I already told you that I wasn't moving in with her.

My dad staggered to his feet. His eyes blazing with fury. "I don't care what you don't want. You are going to live with us until you turn eighteen. Then you get to choose who you want to live with." He took me by the shoulders, applying pressure. The smell of alcohol made me sick to my stomach. Mine wasn't even that bad. My fists were balled up at my side, as I fought the urge to grab him by the shirt collar and toss him off the balcony. "Get inside now. We are out of here at nine. No later!" I broke away from him and slammed the door behind me when I entered the apartment.

I grabbed myself a beer from the fridge and beat the crap out of the wall when I was in the safety of my room.

How dare he bring that woman into our house! My mom would have still been alive if he hadn't had cheated on her! This was beyond disrespectful. When my knuckles were bloody, I plopped down on my bed and crashed.

The next morning, I was rudely awoken by the sound of Mindy and her stupid blinder. I imagined myself strangling the crap out of her and shoving her freshly manicured hand into the damn blinder. I laughed into my pillow at the thought of her blood spattering my face. That was my mother's blinder, and it would have made my mom proud.

My door swung open, smashing into the wall with my father's pinned to it only angered me again. I couldn't even enjoy my fantasy land. " Wake up sunshine!"

I groaned and dragged myself out of bed. When he had his back to me, I flipped him off. I sluggishly made my way over to the closet and snagged the first clothing items that I could find, a pair of skinny jeans and my favorite skull shirt. My boxers seemed fresh still, so I didn't bother. I got myself a steaming shower and took my heavenly time washing off just to piss him off.

Mindy loaded the boxes down with items from the kitchen and sealed them with tape while we did the heavy lifting too and got them into the moving truck. When the kitchen was all packed up, she made us some grilled cheese sandwiches with tomato soup. That was like the only food that she didn't burn.

How my mom found out about Mindy was after a night of screwing around with my father, she burnt some oatmeal on the stove and the police department alerted her. She found him comforting Mindy on the front lawn.

After a long day's work, I locked myself up in my room and checked my email. My heart sank to the pit of my stomach when I didn't receive any alerts from my inbox about Mindy. I scrolled over to her profile picture and clicked on it. Her profile popped up. I checked her feed. There was nothing new since the party.

Just freaking great.

I settled for scrolling through her photos. She had one that stood out from the rest. Her lips were covered with black lipstick. She had a red sweater and a black, lace choker on. Juan whatever his last name was had his arms snaked around her waist. He had her ear between his teeth, she was blushing a smiling like an idiot. I gritted my teeth, squeezing the crap out of the mouse, imagining it was that loser's neck.

Why was this still on here? The guy dropped out of school and I hadn't even seen him around town lately.

I cringed at the memory of them all hugged up at the new year's party that Arianna threw our freshman year.

If anyone was going to be hugged up next to her, it sure as hell was going to be me. I would make her forget all about that low life soon enough.

I couldn't resist the urge to scroll through their old messages to see if there was even the slightest indication of where the jerk disappeared to. I think it was April when he checked out. There were no comments on any of the pictures on the first but the fifth.

The picture was of a quote that said, "Darkness is always waiting to pounce when you're out frolicking around in joy." He commented.

Juan: You need to explain to me what's going on. We said that we would do this. I can't do this without you. Call me.

I wonder what he's referring to. If he was going to leave the next day, what they possibly have been plotting. Oh, well his loss was my gain. I spun my desk chair around and was about to go to bed, but the curiosity was potent. I went and typed his name into the search engine. I was stunned to find him linked up with some other girl. I scrolled down to his friends' list and clicked on her name which was Brittany Hilliard.

She was a little on the plump side but had a pretty face. She was a brunette with a pierced brow. She was almost albino white. Her hair was butch, and she had brown eyes and a dimple near the left corner of her mouth. She lived in California. Juan wasn't the kind to have a long-distance relationship. Sure enough, I verified his location when I checked his profile. His evolution went from posting depressing posts to posting more pictures of himself and posting savage quotes directed toward his ex. He never called her out once.

Little pansy. If he ever said any of this garbage to her, I would tear him to pieces.

I went to sleep that night imagining her lying next to me, stroking my face. The smell of her lavender perfume lingered in my nostrils and her face was etched into my mind. I couldn't wait to make her mine.

Chapter Four

ARES

School was back in session and I was ready to get my hands dirty. That sculpture wasn't going to finish itself. I grabbed myself an energy drink and started making my way toward the art building when I spotted Erik chatting up Samora and Arianna again.

We hadn't planned anything. What the heck does he think he's doing?

 I walked over. Samora's eyes lit up when I did. That made me smile on the inside. I planted a firm hand on Erik's shoulder. "What do you think you're doing? Haven't you had enough tormenting people for a lifetime?"

"So, protective." Arianna giggled. " He was just telling us about this new movie that has come to theaters."

Is that how you want to play it? I dare you to put a finger on Samora. I will take you out right here.

"Did you want to join us?" Arianna asked. I kind of wished that it had come from Samora. I knew she was shy, so I didn't dwell on it too long.

"If I'm not busy. I'm helping my dad move into his girlfriend's house." I lowered my gaze, smirking on the inside. One thing I knew about chicks was the fact that they were suckers for tortured souls.

Samora gasped. "He has a girlfriend already?"

"Yeah. She is the reason why my mom got depressed and took her own life." I frowned.

"Now you must come with us. You are an extraordinarily strong person to take it so lightly. I would be mad as hell." Erik chimed in.

"It's not like I can change anything. My father is a grown man and will do whatever he wants. He doesn't hesitate to remind me daily." I stuffed my hands into the pockets of my jeans, with a hopeless look on my face.

"We should all meet up at Samora's house and then take my car to get there," Arianna suggested. I had to give her a round of applause. She deserved wingman of the year. I just had to see if Samora would pick up on what she was throwing down. I started gnawing on the inside of my cheek, waiting for a response.

"We can't. My dad will kill me if he sees two guys in the yard." She frowned.

"Your place is closer to the theater." Erik encouraged.

How the hell did he know where she lived? Most importantly, why did he not tell me!

"We can park in the alley." Was my suggestion.

Arianna linked her arm through Samora's and poked out her lip. "You know that you can live a little. Throw out the past and get with the present."

"If I get caught, my dad will never let me out of the house again." She sighed.
"You know that he's still sensitive about certain things."

What I loved about her was that she was cryptic. It made the hunt even more satisfying. I couldn't wait to break her barrier and unleash the beast within. I needed to calm myself before my lower appendage betrayed me.

"Fine."

The bell suddenly rang, and I let the others walk ahead of me. I was walking on air. This would be our first date and I was going to find out where she lived. Moves were going to be made. I just needed another game plan and to have a chat with Erik the scumbag.

During ceramics, I couldn't stop watching her through the corner of my eye. I loved watching her channel her heart and soul into something. Mr. Gold let everyone who'd completed their sculptures have a free day. She was making clay flowers.

That day I was in the process of sculpting the arms of my mother holding onto her broken Heart. That was the simple portion of the process. All I had to do was roll the arms out and remove access clay. Then I would go in with the sculpting tool for the fingers.

My phone started buzzing. When I went to unlock the phone there was a message from Erik. The little pansy was probably trying to avoid a face-to-face confrontation.

Erik: Before you get all accusatory, I have always had a thing for Arianna. I'm not into prudes.

This bastard had some nerve calling my future girlfriend a prude. If he were in my face, I would have stomped his body into the gravel.

Ares: Well, you and I are supposed to be enemies, so tonight be prepared for a Kick-Ass time.

Two seconds later, my phone went off again.

Erik: what do you mean by that?

Ares: just wait and see.
I snickered.

"Uh Maybe... Ares." Samora cleared her throat.

My head shot up really quick. " What's up?"

"I couldn't help but notice that you and Erik seem to be on better terms. Before you showed up" she rubbed the back of her neck, awkwardly. " I kind of told him to lay off." She sort of laughed. She was too adorable.

"Oh, you didn't have to. I still hate his guts, but if suffering through him is what I have to do to hang with friends then it's a price I'm willing to make." I pulled up my contacts and asked her to type in her number. Those caramel cheeks turned a light pink.

When she handed the phone back to me, I sent her a text asking her for her address. They went from pink to cherry red. I couldn't help but smile. After the address, she sent me a reminder to park out in the alley. I sent her, can't wait. I could see her bite down on her bottom lip. It was amazing how easily she could turn me on.

Stay focused! This is not the place or the time!

I fought the urge to ask her if she would like to join me for lunch before class was dismissed. I told myself that I was being greedy and there would plenty of time with her after tonight. The plan that I came up with was full proof.

School seemed to drag out. My mind was stuck on her the whole time. I could barely concentrate. I couldn't stop imagining my head buried in her chest. I could almost smell the lavender body spray. I found myself excusing myself from class to splash some cold water on my face.

When school was out, I avoided home like the plague. I drove out to her house and parked in the alleyway. I was an hour carly, but that didn't matter to me. That meant I got extra time to scope out the territory.

I stepped out of the car and found a hole in the fence that gave me a good view of the backyard. It was a pretty decent size. No dogs either. I pictured her sneaking me in through the back gate and the backdoor.

When Erik drove up with Arianna in the passengers' seat. I backed away from the gate. After they stepped out, Arianna shot me a quizzical look. " were you spying?" She playfully nudged me in the arm.

"I thought I heard her coming out."

Great cover-up.

The next thing I knew the back gate swung open and the awkward vanished. She came out in a black dress with some roses scattered about the bottom. The collar was shaped like a V, accenting her chest perfectly. That gorgeous hair was in curls and that caramel complexion seemed to glow. A gentle breeze blew through those curls sending a tropical fragrance to my nostrils. She surely knew how to get my heart racing.

She caught me staring, tucked her hair behind her ear and those cheeks turned red. "You guys ready?" She shifted her gaze from me to them.

" Let's do this thing!" Arianna hoped back into the car, I caught Erik with the same jaw-dropped expression on his face. My fist was just itching to contact that dumb face of his. I had to be on my best behavior for now. On the drive over, I called in a favor from a guy who would guarantee me a night in those succulent breasts.

Samora hopped into the car with me, and we took off down the alley. I looked over at her and almost rammed my car into Erik's. He honked the horn like the jackass he was, and I honked back in the same agitated manor.

"Are you alright?"

Think of something quick that won't tarnish your cool-guy persona.

"I'm just a little tired. That's all."

" Do you want me to drive?"

Way to go dumbass.

" No. I will be fine. Thanks." I frustratedly scratched the top of my head, drawing blood. The sting of it was annoying, I hated starting off the night with a rough start like that. Now I would be wallowing in embarrassment that night before bed. It was funny how one freaking mishap could wreck my entire night. All I wanted was to fucking smooth was that too much to ask?

When we pulled into the parking lot, Erik found a spot a few cars away from the entrance in the third row. Just my luck, we ended up circling the lot three times before a blue pickup truck backed out of a spot in the fifth row at the very end. I apologized to her for that one. As we made our way to the entrance of the building, I pulled out my phone and informed the guy that we were at the theater now. That way when I gave him the go-ahead, he would already be in the venue. He sent me a thumbs up and we cashed in at the register.

She retrieved her wallet from her purse and asked for a large popcorn and some licorice. "You don't have to pay. It's on me." There she went blushing again. I could just eat her up. I paid for her stuff and bought us each a large coke and a box of chocolate drops.

Let the games begin!

We came just in time. I was pissed when Arianna rushed ahead of Erik. That meant that Samora would be seated between Erik and me.

I will chop off that hand of yours If I see you trying to do the stereotypical guy move tonight.

"Thanks back there. You didn't have to buy me anything."

"I wanted to. It was the least that I could do after you helped scrape my sculpture off the floor."

I could feel her eyes on me throughout the movie. The corner of my mouth raised. Things were moving too damn slow. A few minutes into the film, I started getting extremely anxious. I wanted to feel that warm body against mine and taste those luscious lips now! My heart was pounding, and I was losing circulation in my hand from squeezing too tight. I whipped out my phone and shot the guy the okay. Suddenly popcorn started raining down on us from behind. I sprang up from my seat. People were voicing their protests and I put on my game face and turned to face my fake oppressor.

Jeremy Sterling was his name. He and I had been friends since kindergarten. Now we were just acquaintances. He owed me money, so I offered to let the bastard off the hook with this simple task.

"What the hell man!" My brows furrowed and my jaw was clenched. The wrath of Satan was blazing in my eyes.

"It was a freaking accident. Calm the hell down."

" Apologize to Samora now!" Erik joined in.

Samora tugged on my jacket telling me that it was okay and asked me to sit down.

"Not until this bastard apologizes." My fists were balled up against my sides.

" Take her advice and sit the hell down!" The people in the theater were started to chant sit down over and over again. My blood was literally boiling at that point.

"You and me, outside now!" He shot up out of his seat and flung Icy soda all over my clothes. He rushed towards the end of the row. Erik gave him a good punch in the stomach before I could even get there.

Both of these bastards were going to die.

I grabbed a fist full of Erik's hair and jerked him out the damn way. Then Jeremy delivered a jaw-cracking punch to my face. I staggered backward and popped it back into place while Erik charged at his stomach, knocking him straight into the trashcan that emptied its contents all over the burgundy floor. That drew a crowd fast. Erik was stealing my moment whaling on Jeremy. Arianna broke out her cellphone recording the entire thing. Samora was trying to pull Erik off of Jeremy. It was a fucking disaster. To make matters worse, the ushers stepped in and broke the fight up. After we were escorted off the premises, Samora stopped me in my tracks on the way to the car and looked me over. She reached into her purse and took out some tissue. "You're bleeding." She dabbed my bottom lip. I was so caught up in the adrenaline rush that it didn't start stinging until she said something.

Before I got the car started, I heated things by removing my drenched shirt and tossed it into the trunk of the car. I heard her draw in a sharp breath. She hid behind her phone, fighting the urge to look. I hit the gym quite often, so I had plenty to show off. I might not have been a gorilla, but my arms were ripped, and I had a six-pack.

You know you want to look. I dare you too. You really are falling for me. Just say the word and we can take this friendship to the next level. I want you to slide that tongue down my torso and show me what the real Samora is like. I found myself strangling the steering wheel, fighting the beast within from being exposed too quickly. I bit down on my bottom lip. The pain was enough to put the beast down for a nap.

"Did they say where we were going?" I asked, slicking my hair back.

"Let me call Arianna really quick." She pulled out her phone. Arianna answered after the second ring.

"Where are we heading?" She put her on speaker.

"Erik thought since the sun was setting that we could chill on the park with some booze."

"That sounds fun." She leaned her head against the window. Man, If only it would have been my shoulder instead.

When we reached the park, we hung out in the graffitied flood tunnels that were on the dry end of the pond. It was empty looking, so Erik passed out the flashlights. Arianna was in the lead holding Erik's hand. Samora held his other. When our hands touched an electric current surged throughout my entire body. Every hair on me stood on end from the intensity. Judging from the way she looked back at me and the color of her cheeks, it must have been the same for her.

We stopped somewhere down the middle and got settled. I had to sweep away some dried-up weeds with my foot before sitting down. Arianna had to be a fucking buzz kill and squeeze between Samora and me, on the opposite side of where we sat. Erik stepped over me and took the other side as well. We were now facing each other.

He pulled his backpack off and distributed the alcohol. We started out with beer before he brought out the whiskey bottle. "So, how did you find out about this place?" Arianna asked.

"When Ares and I were kids, we would come down here and tag up the walls with spray paint. Our staff should be down here somewhere."

"Awe that's too cool."

"What now?" Samora asked.

"How about a game of truth or dare?" She could never resist a game of truth or dare.

"How juvenile of you." I rolled my eyes.

"Since you are all moody, you can go first. What will it be truth or dare?"

"Dare. I'm. Not a freaking pansy." With that being said, he dared me to strip off my pants and flash everyone.

The corner of my mouth rose. "Is there something you want to tell me?"

"Don't flatter yourself. I just have always suspected that you were tiny." Those were challenging words. It was a little chilly down there but hey if that would make him shut that stupid mouth of his. I stood up and pulled them down. His eyes were the size of bowling balls and his mouth was gaping wide open. If I wcrc a dirtbag, I would have slapped him in the face with it. Samora's eyes were covered to my disappointment. Arianna on the other hand was eyeing it as If was the holy grail with her lips pressed against the rim of the whiskey bottle. I pulled my pants back up and took a seat.

"Who's small?" I laughed. " Truth or dare?"

"Dare." He said, glowering.

Time for revenge. " I dare you to kiss Arianna." He shrugged and we swapped spots so that he could get in there and I could reclaim my spot next to Samora. Just when he was about to lean in, "using tongues." I just had to add. Arianna looked away, placing a hand over his mouth, and then drank some more booze before proceeding. Samora and I got a real kick out of that one.

That would keep him away from my woman. Arianna was the first to break away. " Okay, truth or dare." She went for truth. He looked so freaking disappointed; it was hilarious.

"Is it true that you made out with coach Green during the basketball game last year?" I was surprised that her cheeks turned bright red.

That guy was about thirty years old, had a mole that protruded from the side of his neck, and had a fork nose with beady eyes and paper-thin lips. The corner of his mouth was always twitching. He was balding for crying out loud.

Everyone gasped. "I can't believe you."

" Yeah." Erik wrinkled his nose. "I wasn't expecting that." He reached over her and took three huge gulps from the whiskey bottle.

"Hey, he is a pretty good kisser."

"I doubt that. With his twitchy mouth." We all laughed.

Her eyes shot over to Samora thirsting for blood. "Truth or dare?" Samora stopped laughing. "Dare."

Alcohol made that girl bold.

"I dare you to make out with Ares!"

I loved bitchy Arianna. She became my new best friend. The beast was armed and ready to play now.

"With pleasure." She climbed right into my lap, facing me. I had a hard-on really bad. There was no way she couldn't notice it. She entangled those fingers into my hair and went in for the kill. I didn't wait for her to meet me halfway, I captured that bottom lip of hers and penetrated those plump lips with my tongue, forgetting about the audience. I had never felt the urge to be so close to someone that I wanted to have sex with their soul before. When the kiss was over, our foreheads were pressed together, breathing each other's air.
There was nothing but silence for a while. Then her phone had to go and vibrate in her back pocket. She got off of me moments before I erupted.

"Alright. I'm on my way home now." When I parked the car in the alley, I walked her to the gate.

"I'll see you tomorrow." I had my hands stuffed in my pockets, rocking back and forth on my heels, hating to see her go.

"Yeah." She awkwardly looked down at her feet. " Thanks for the ride." When she left, it felt like she took my oxygen with her. I lingered in the alley and watched her bedroom light cut on before I drove away. After something as magical as that, I was even more determined to have her.

Chapter Five

Samora

I woke up with a crazy hangover. The sun was beating down on my face. I took a stretch and dragged myself out of bed.

"Samora! It's time to get up." My dad shouted from the other side of the door.

"I'm up." I walked over sluggishly moved over to the closet and grabbed comfort clothes. Which consisted of sweatpants and a blue T-Shirt. I threw my hair up in a messy bun and covered my face with base makeup and brown eyeshadow. I knew that crap would get messed up if I tried to use liner. The last time I attempted to use eyeliner with a hangover, I stabbed myself in the freaking eye.

When I got downstairs, I made myself some toast and spread some grape jelly over it before heading out. I wasn't going to lie; I had a mad case of butterflies. After that steaming make-out session with Ares, I hoped to God that if he didn't want to turn our friendship into something more that he didn't treat me like a jerk about it. I didn't really know where his mind was. Sometimes he was incredibly quiet and other times, outgoing. Then he seemed like he was open to a relationship then he was closed off and chasing Megan.

When I stepped out of the car, he had just hit the bumper to his. "Oh, hey." He waved. I was not ready for this crap, this damn early in the morning.

"I think we should talk about last night." He laughed nervously and rubbed the back of his neck.

Here it goes. Shoot me now!

"Alright. Where did you want to go?" I checked the time on my phone. We had some time to kill, sadly.

"How about behind D building?" That was where the stoners hung out.

"Are you sure that's the best place to talk in private?"

"Don't worry. The coast is clear."

I cocked a brow. "How do you know?"

"Because I scoped it out before you showed up."

I guess he could have forgotten something in his car.

Once we were in the safety of the back of the D building, he leaned against the wall and asked me what my thoughts were about the event that transpired between us. In other words.

Why do you have to ask me? The ball is in your court. I already have feelings for you. Your answer will determine whether I reveal them to you.

"I wasn't freaked out about it." That was all I gave him.

"That kiss had some kick to it. Don't you agree?"

Now my cheeks were blazing. "So, what do you want from me?"

Maybe those weren't the right choice of words. He looked at me with hurt plagued eyes.

"I don't expect anything of you. I just wanted to know If things were cool between us." He kept his eyes on the ground. When I didn't respond, he got this stubborn look on his face and marched over to me. He entangled his finger through my hair and pressed those deliciously smooth lips on mine, forcing his bottom lip between mine. I could have died from how intense it all was. His hand slid down my back. I broke away from him, feeling dizzy and breathless. He looked the way I felt.

The bell rang and he took me by the hand on the way over to the art building. I didn't expect things to progress this fast. I needed time to think. This guy was fire to me. If I didn't cool down, I would combust. The last time that I lost control, I became the black sheep of the family. My dad literally called up everyone. Thankfully, my father didn't know everything, or Juan might not have made it out of town.

Mr. Gold distributed fresh clay to everyone that day. He told us that he wanted to see what we could accomplish on our own. That was my favorite part of the class. Once I got it where It was pliable, I started writing down ideas into my notebook. When nothing cool came to mind at first, I just sat there, on the brink of drooling over Ares and the way his muscles looked when he slammed clay down and a drop of sweat slid down his gorgeous face.

I leaned my cheek on my hand, marveling. That was all fun and games until Mr. Gold interrupted. " You are brainstorming or gawking at Ares?" I quickly jotted down the word wolf.

"I think you have some pretty cool ideas. Now show me what you're capable of." He gave me a pat on the back. I caught a glimpse of Ares smiling.

Kill me now.

When lunchtime came around, I spotted my father coming from. The main office. I didn't know what to think. My chest started tightening. I rushed over to him, scaring him half to death. "What are you doing here?"

" Oh, I just went in to update my contact information. I broke my phone at work. I figured that since it was my lunch break, I could get it over with. He held out his hand. " Let me give you the new number."

I reached into my pocket and handed my phone over. I never anticipated my phone going off and the call coming from Ares.

His brows pulled together. " What's this boy doing on your phone?" He lifted the phone so I could see.

" He's just a friend." Spewed out of my mouth. That didn't wipe his suspicious look from his face. He typed in the number and took off.

Great. Now I must endure yet another one of his stupid lectures.

Arianna dragged me off to the courtyard. "We need to talk about what went down last night in the tunnel." She took a seat on the grass and set her bag down next to her. I took a seat mirroring her.

"What is there to talk about? I was drunk." I started plucking the grass in front of me.

Her eyes widened. " Are you being serious right now! You kissed Ares, a little too enthusiastically if you ask me. I thought you guys were going to start stripping each other."

"Well, you know how I feel about him, so it's not a surprise."

"What did he say about it?"

"He kissed me again." Why was it that just acknowledging it out loud aroused me a little?

"Are you guys dating?"

"I don't think so." I didn't like the sound of that, but it was the truth.

Erik found us at one of the tables beneath the shade of a tree. He plopped his backpack down on the table and asked me how I was feeling.

"I'm fine. Why do you ask?"

He opened his milk carton and took a drink. "Do you have any memory of what went down in the tunnel yesterday?"

" Oh, please." Ares took a seat next to me, scaring the living daylights out of me while doing so. My cheeks were heating up to the point of boiling off my face.

"Are you guys a thing?" Arianna sounded a little too hopeful.

"Are you and Erik a thing?" He shot back at her. She shifted her gaze down to her chicken nuggets and took a bite of one.

I wanted an answer. I just didn't want to be in the same venue when he gave it. A text would have sufficed.

Later, that afternoon when I got home, my father called me into the kitchen. Steam was surfacing from the thick, juicy steak that was sizzling on the skillet. He jabbed it with a meat fork and flipped it over. The steam intensified and the sizzling grew louder.

"Where did you meet this guy?"

"He is one of my classmates." I slid out a chair and took a seat at the table.

"I don't want a repeat of what happened the last time. Do you understand me?" He turned off the stove and took a plate down from the cabinet to put the steak on. The smell of seasoning was mouthwatering.

My mind was not ready to go back to that earth-shattering moment. I gritted my teeth, trying to fight it off. The candlelit bathroom and the sound of rushing water were where I put a stop to it.

"You don't have to worry. We're just friends." I said curtly.

"You'd better not be lying to me." He set his plate down on the table and sawed away.

"I promise you that I'm not." My eyes began to flood, and I could no longer fight the urge to swallow.

I grabbed myself a granola bar from the pantry and bottled water from the fridge. Then rushed upstairs to my room for the remainder of the day.

At two in the morning, I was restless and so I went downstairs to make myself a sandwich. As I was retrieving the meat from the fridge, I heard a metal sound coming from the back fence. My heart froze in my chest.

Could someone be trying to break in?

I slowly slid the glass doors open, not making too much of a sound, and cautiously and very stealthily made my way to the fence. There was a tiny peephole that you could see through. I thought maybe if I looked through it, I could make out what was on the other side. The fence started shaking violently and I stopped in my tracks. I cupped my hand over my mouth the muffle the scream that threatened to escape my mouth. Suddenly my father stepped out onto the patio.

" What are you doing out here, so late?" Then the sound of shoes against the dirt tapered off down the alley. I quickly rushed over and opened the gate. All I saw was a glimpse of a male figure about six-foot running in a black hoodie and matching jeans. My father came out after me.

"Someone was trying to break in." I cried into his chest.

"Did you get a good look at him?"
I told him everything about him. " Well, I'm glad that you came out here when you did. I can go down to the police station tomorrow and file a report."

Long story short, I didn't sleep a wink that night.

That was close. Too damn close. I laid on my bed, panting drenched in sweat.

What the hell was I thinking? I should have been stealthier. My dad knocked on my door. I quickly got up to answer it.

"What up?"

"Tomorrow we are moving the last of our stuff into the other house alright. You had better come straight home, or you won't have one to come back to."

"Yeah. Whatever." I rolled my eyes and shut the door. I stripped down to my boxers and slept like a baby.

The next day, my alarm went off. I reached over and shut it off. I climbed out of bed and dragged myself over to the closet for some clothes. I found a shirt lying on the floor that had a zombie face on it and a pair of skinny Jeans. I didn't bother changing boxers. I wasn't getting laid anytime soon. After hopping into the shower, I sprayed myself down with cologne and rolled on some fresh deodorant, and was out the door before Mindy could stop me and force me to eat breakfast with her and my dad. The only thing in life that I wanted more than anything was to taste Samora's lips again.

I hopped into the car and took off down the street. My phone started buzzing. I reached into my backpack and opened the message. It was a text from my dad, sending one last reminder to go straight home after school. I rolled my eyes and tossed the phone into the passenger's seat.

I honestly didn't care if I didn't have a home to come back to. Mindy could jump off the nearest cliff and I could sleep in my car. It was already paid off, so I didn't care. I could go get myself a job and save up for an apartment.

After I got the car parked, I spotted the one that I wanted, sitting underneath the shade of the tree that I liked to hang out under before class. She looked worried and who was I to deny her a shoulder to cry on. I walked over and took a seat in front of her in the grass.

"What's wrong?" Those gorgeous brown eyes were flooding.

"Do you think that we ever truly get free from our past?" A tear escaped the corner of her eye. I reached over and dried it before she could. To see her cheeks, turn red like that just made my freaking day.

"I think that you can just replace the bad crap with good memories and then the bad memories won't bother you so much anymore." That put a glimmer of hope in her eye.

Stupid Juan was going to pay for whatever damage he'd done when she opened up enough to tell me what it was that she was trying to escape from.

"Thanks for saying that." She smiled. "I just get so depressed that I don't know how to deal with life. I feel so alone and hopeless when my past comes to bite me in the ass." She sighed.

"Well, it was my pleasure. Feel free to open up to me anytime you need to." I smiled.

" Thanks again."

My phone went off once more. I rose from the ground and answered it on the fourth ring when I was out of earshot. It was a call from Megan. " What do you want?" I groaned.

"Why are you being like that? I told you that I wanted a second chance, and you blew me off." I hated hearing the hurt in her voice.

"I told you that I've been busy."

"Well, are you free this afternoon? I want to speak with you face to face."

My brows furrowed. "I thought you would have gone back home by now." I frustratedly scratched the top of my head, on the brink of having a meltdown.

"Seeing you at that party the other day made me realize that I still want to be with you. I'm moving back." I couldn't get the girl of my dreams if Megan were clinging onto me. Just fantastic.

The bell rang. "Listen, I have to go. The bell just rang, and I can't be late." I started heading back toward the art building.

"Don't forget to call me, alright." I hung up the phone and shoved it into my pocket.

When I walked into class, Mr. Gold was waiting for me by the door. "I have been impressed with your work lately." He handed me a pamphlet that was for an art competition at the college. " The winner will receive a dollar prize. If you're interested?" That sounded great. I could use the cash.

"That sounds awesome. I will definitely look into it." I grinned. Then took my seat. I was finished with the statue and I needed to make something spectacular that would knock the socks off the judges.

I slid my desk over to Samora's and asked her how she felt about being my muse for the competition. Those cheeks were extremely red and her eyes wide. "You want me to be your muse?"

"If that isn't too much to ask?" I gave her my best puppy dog look. She was smiling so hard that she had to look away. I stumbled into phase two of my journey to winning her heart.

"Okay?" She nervously bit the corner of her bottom lip. That was enough to get my heart pumping. Had to stay focused. This was a classroom for crying out loud.

"So, what do you need me to do?" She leaned her hand on her cheek. That was perfect. I took out my phone and walked over to the front of her desk. She looked confused.

"Just sit like that." I took a picture of her and saved it on my phone. Then went back to my seat. "Perfect." The gears started turning. I needed something to represent what she meant to me. It had you have sentimental value as well. To me, she was a swan amongst geese The unicorn amongst the black stallions. I decided to give her a unicorn horn, wings, a swan necklace, and etch stars into her arms. I started messing around with photoshop and came up with the rough sketch later during lunch. When I showed it to her, she lit up like the fourth of July. I was even more determined after that.

Sadly, instead of making my escape to the damn library, my dad was waiting for me in the lot. "What are you doing here?" I jerked my car door open and took a seat.

"I'm making sure that you go directly home this afternoon. We only have three days to vacate, and I will be damned if I let you stand in the way of my happiness." He slammed his fist down on the hood of the car. I could have punched him out right then and there, but what good would that have done? I would have landed myself behind bars and would never accomplish anything. I needed art as much as breathing and this bastard only cared about his happiness. I slammed the car door and followed him out to our place.

The first thing that we loaded up into the moving truck was my dad's bed and stuffed all his three-piece suit trash bags. Then the heavy lifting began. We took the mattress down first then the box spring and lastly the bed frame and headboard. The last thing to leave his room was the portable wooden dresser in front of the window. When we took a break, I checked my phone and found some unopened messages from Megan. When I opened them, I instantly regretted it. She was naked and flashing her chest at me. Then another one came in, saying maybe that would remind me of all the fun times we shared with a winking emoji. I couldn't breathe. She had me there. I needed to delete them and fast. I hesitated with the last one. She was sucking on a red sucker and her lips looked incredibly irresistible. Then I remembered my master plan and deleted it. I sent her a message, telling her not to send me that shit ever again.

I would have been better off ignoring her. She started asking me why I didn't love her anymore and pointing out all the reasons why we should be together. I shut my phone off and stepped out onto the balcony for some fresh air.

My dad came out to light up. When he released the huge cloud of smoke, there went my fresh air. "You seem distracted lately? You are tapping a new girl?"

"As if I would tell you." I stepped over to the railing, to get away from all that smoke.

" You see, that's your problem. You keep chasing girls and you aren't focused on the big picture. If you don't watch out, you might get yourself killed. Women are great and all, but some can be a real nuisance."

What did he know about the big picture? I could sculpt for a damn living. That was nothing. If there was a freaking will there was a damn way.

"I've got a clear view of the big picture. Today in ceramics Mr. Gold thought that I had enough potential to enter my work into a competition down at the college. I have the women right where I want them. As if that's any of your business."

"Well, I hope it all works out for you. I know that you've got talent because you get that from your mom. I just want you to stay focused and work hard so that in the future if something were to happen to me, you can take care of yourself."

"Don't worry about me old man. I am already capable of that."

"Alright. Break time's over." He clapped. I followed him back inside to finish up. We got out of there around six. When everything was put away, we dined on Mindy's stupid lasagna that she heated in the oven the edges were a little burnt but that was nothing I could rinse my taste buds off with beer. That was literally the only thing about growing up with my dad that I could appreciate.

The next day, I slaved away over beating the clay into shape and getting off to a decent start. With the right heavy metal blasting from my earbuds and determination, I managed to get the head carved out by the following day. It felt so damn great to channel all my energy into something I loved. I had to be just as aggressive when it came to Samora. I needed her so badly I would die without her.

Chapter Six

Samora

Just watching Ares hollow out the head of the sculpture and that look of determination was intoxicating. I loved how he put his everything into his work. It made my heart pound. If he could put so much of himself into something that he loved, I couldn't even imagine how much love he would put into a relationship with someone that he deemed worthy of his heart. I could watch him all day.

The class was over too soon. I needed some more time with him. I just didn't know how to go about it. He made me his muse and kissed me twice. What was so difficult about inviting him out somewhere. Hell, I didn't even know where I wanted to go with him. How lame was I?

He walked me to my next class. I stopped at the door. "Are you busy this afternoon?" Spewed out of my mouth before I could think my way into having a brain aneurysm.

"No. Did you have something in mind?" I got a huge lump in my throat and couldn't piece sentences together in my mind to form words. " How about we discuss this at lunch?"

"Okay." I entered the classroom, beating my palm against my forehead. Why was it that during the times that I wanted to be bold, I ended up making a huge fool of myself?

I took my seat next to Arianna who asked me what the heck happened just now. "I tried to ask him out but then I couldn't figure out where the heck I wanted to take him, and my brain totally shut down." I buried my face in my arms, dying of shame.

"Well, what did he say?"

"He wanted to talk about it during lunch." I groaned.

"He wants to go out with you. This is freaking fantastic! You are about to strike gold, my friend. You guys already planted your lips on each other. Pretty soon you will be going on your first date. Tonight! Fingers crossed." She squealed.

"What if neither of us can come up with somewhere to go? Sometimes he is silent as hell. This could be a huge disaster." I lifted my head to the sound of the tardy bell.

"Now you're overthinking it. Calm down and let the good vibes flow. The less you think the better off you will be. You already got him on the damn hook. Reel his ass in already."

Lunchtime came too soon. I went in blind. He captured me by the arm and asked me if I would like to go to the Club Of Mirrors. That sounded a little nerve-wracking, but he came up with it, so how was I to refuse?

The place was not too far from school. It was had a five-star rating and a hell of a lot of privacy. There was a restaurant, an arcade a bar, and a lounge that was sectioned off for intimate interaction. My dad's head would have exploded if he found out that I went there on my lunch break, but I didn't want to seem like a pansy In front of the coolest guy that ever took interest in me.

I was sweating bullets on the way over. We took his car. He had a nice tropical scented air freshener hanging from the mirror and a silver skull necklace. It must have been nice to drive to school every day in that thing.

When we reached our destination, he walked around the car and opened the door for me. I stepped out and he placed a gentle hand on my back as we approached the building. The place had mirrored walls and ceilings. The tables were mirror topped with iron frames and the chairs had oval-shaped mirrors on the back with golden frames. The booths had fancy flower arrangements in the center of each table. The regular tables had miniature Grecian statues in the center. The place was buzzing with all walks of life. A waitress at the front counter asked where we would like to dine.

He whispered something in her ear and that was a tad unsettling. She nodded and a grin spread across her face. She grabbed two menus from under the counter a d lead us toward the back of the room through huge doors with leafy vines etched into the glass. When we stepped behind that door, we found ourselves down a narrow hallway that reminded me of looking into a kaleidoscope doorknob She opened the second door on the right and we found ourselves in one of the private lounge areas. Each one had a coffee table with a half-circle-shaped couch with hallow pillows.

"What can you guys to drink?"

"I will have a coke and what will you have?" He led me over to the couch where I took a seat. I didn't really like coke all that well, but I was so nervous and fidgety I said I would have the same.

"Today special menu items are half off." She passed out the menus.

I looked it over and spotted the baked pasta shells with spinach ricotta cheese. I ordered that and he ordered the chicken stir fry. I made sure that it was one of the special menu items so that I didn't feel guilty about him overspending. While we waited for the food to arrive, he asked me what I thought about the place.

"It's really impressive. I have never seen anything like it my entire life." I smiled.

"I have an uncle who works as a financial advisor for this place, so I get discounts on all the arcade games and food regardless." He grinned.

"Aren't you full of surprises?"

"I was glad that you asked me out. I have been so wrapped up in my art that I kind of forgets how to be involved in the real world. I apologized for that. You must have thought I was a prick for not asking you out sooner."

"Never," I said curtly. The waitress returned with our drinks and food. After she set everything down, she told us to press a button located under the surface of the table and she would get back to us as soon as possible. Then she told us to enjoy and left us to our own devices.

Each bite melted on my tongue. I was in sheer bliss. To kill the silence, I asked him how the movie was coming along. He took a sip of coke. "I hate it, but the move Is officially over. Mindy is over the moon about it and so is my dad. I just hate leaving the home that I have all those memories in with my mom."

"That must be terrible to have to leave it all behind like that."

" It really is. You should come to check out the new house this afternoon and tell me what you think." I was in the middle of drinking when he said that and started choking. He quickly gave me a pat on the back and asked if it was too sudden.

"Just unexpected." I cleared my throat and set my glass down on the table.

"Would you feel better if I threw a house party instead? It might take the pressure off."

He certainly knew how to blow me away. " If that's alright with you."
He pursed his lips and gave me a nod. I felt so rude.

" How about I throw one this weekend?"

"Sounds fun." I chewed. Before we both knew it, we were rushing out of there as if the place were on fire. He weaved in and out of traffic just to make it on time, but despite his efforts, the bell rang as soon as we stepped out of the car. We were sent straight to detention for an entire class period.

When I got home that afternoon, my father was livid. "What were you doing leaving campus for lunch with a boy in the first place?" He had his arms folded standing on the front porch. I didn't even get inside before sparks started flying.

"He just took me out for a meal. Nothing else." I whined.

"Is he your boyfriend?"

He never asked to be my boyfriend, so I hated to admit that he was just a friend. It was what it was though. "He is just an art friend."

"Well, make sure that your friend is prepared for me to meet him and his parents tomorrow." He marched into the house. I shut the door behind us and ran upstairs to scream into a pillow and beat my fists on the bed. We weren't even a couple yet and my dad wanted to meet the guy's parents. I hated that one little mistake changed everything for my dad when it came to me being anywhere near the make species. He now assumed that all of them just wanted to sleep with me. I hated it so much.

I didn't even know how I was to go about asking him if it would be alright for our parents to meet. I would be pissed off if our relationship ended before it even began. I didn't want him to assume that I was the clingy psychopath who jumped the gun and scares the hottest guy in school off.

I found his profile online and thought that would be the way to go. Why the heck was I even doing this. No! There was no way in hell I was going to jeopardize what we had like that. I sent the message but got offline immediately. I didn't know how I would react if he didn't respond right away.

The following day, Erik spotted me and Arianna me in the courtyard. "So, are you girls going to the party of the century this weekend?"

My dad was asking questions about Ares and his response to the parent meeting over texts when he popped up. I told him that I would have to ask him when I found him on campus. Hopefully, the poor guy got sick or something.

"Ares sent out invitations through email and text about his housewarming party this weekend. Did you get one?" She frowned, frantically through her phone.

"No. Why didn't he invite me?" A boy wearing a letterman jacket who had brown, curly locks and a dimpled smile passed by and said that he couldn't wait to see her at the party.

"Have any of you seen him today?"

"No. He probably is in the art room as we speak." With that being said, she linked arms with me and practically dragged me to the art building.

He nowhere in sight. In fact, no one was in the room. The door was locked, and the lights were off. I still hadn't received a response to my friend either. I was beginning to worry. It would be a real bummer if he didn't show up. I was looking forward to seeing him and seeing what he had in store for me that day. He was like a light switch. One minute he was really invested and then the next, he was kind of shy.

Eventually, the bell for first period rang. It was nice to not have to walk so far. I told Arianna that I would get to the bottom of this if he showed up for school, hugged her, and got out all the supplies that I needed to make a gigantic, monarch butterfly amongst a pot of fake flowers. I already made out the stems and attached leaves. I just needed to make a hollowed-out chunk of clay with holes to place the stems attached to the tops of the flowers and then place one huge butterfly on a stem in the center. The pot would have some sort of fancy designs etched into the pot portion. My goal was to make them look as lifelike as possible.

The last person to step through the door was Ares. I could ask him to Invite Arianna and see if he could respond to my message finally. He slammed down his backpack on his desk, looking like he could murder someone. When he was back at his desk with his wet clay, he didn't even say hello or good morning to me. My heart sank to the pit of my stomach in response.

He slid his backpack off the desk with his elbow and then placed his materials down. " Are you okay?"

"My dad is just being a prick again."

"Are you still throwing a party?"

"With the way, things are going, would you settle for a kickback?"

"I don't mind." He smiled and said, then a kickback it is." He removed the wet paper towels that he'd wrapped the hallowed-out head in and set them on the corner of his desk. Then got straight to work.

When lunch rolled around, my father grew impatient and found me, Arianna, and Ares heading over to the cafeteria. He eyeballed the poor guy up and down, with a mad case of the judge eye.

"You must be the guy who got my daughter detention."

Ares's brows pulled together. My body temperature skyrocketed, and my heart was on the brink of exploding. "I'm Ares. And you are?"

"Samora's father. I'm not sure if she mentioned that I would like to have dinner with your parents this weekend." He gave me a scolding look. I lowered my gaze, feeling the world around me collapse.

So much for getting to know one another better.

"I beg your pardon?" He looked as if someone had just told him that the humus, he thought he'd been eating had turned out to be dog poop.

"There are some things that I would like to discuss with them." My dad pulled out his phone waiting for Ares to give him his contact information.

"I'm afraid that my parents are out of town for the week and won't be home until Tuesday of next week." If he was lying, he was a freaking master at it. Too bad my father was always one step ahead of the current.

"Then I will settle for a phone call." He handed the phone to him. Suddenly principal Edith came strolling out.

"May I ask why you aren't wearing a visitor sticker sir?"

"I was on my way to the front desk to get one when I bumped into my daughter. She was just telling me where to find her English teacher."

"Alright. I will accompany you to the office and get you that visitor's sticker." She smiled and he smiled back. When they walked off, my phone buzzed with a text message from him, saying that this wasn't over. I couldn't help but worry.

"I think I just got myself grounded." I frowned.

"Don't worry. We can try some other time and as for the whole parent thing, I can just give him my grandmother's phone number. She always has her hearing aid turned off when she isn't paying bills." He held out his hand for my phone and sent the number to my dad in a text.

"You crafty bitch." Arianna slapped him in the arm. I was just as amazed.

"We can have the party next weekend. How long do you usually stay grounded for?"

"Normally a week."

"It's settled then." He surprised me by draping his arm around me the rest of the walk to the cafeteria. He smelled like a spice rack in the best possible way. I couldn't wait to get used to this sort of interaction. If things kept going at this rate, If I didn't, I would be hospitalized.

Chapter Seven

Ares

Draping my arm around her felt so damn good, I felt invincible. I didn't want to wait an entire week to be with her again. I needed some way of getting her down from that high horse and out of that damn house Saturday. It was Tuesday when I saw a van parked in the driveway for the security company. There was no way I was going to deal with that garbage. I wanted her to be the one to sneak me in.

After school, I caught her just before she got into her car. " How about you tell your dad that you had to stay after so that we can hang out?" She looked at me and then it faded.

"I'm in enough trouble as it is."

My eyes lingered on those beautiful hands of hers. I bit my lip, trying to stop my mind from them getting tangled up in my hair and our naked bodies giving each other exactly what we had been tiptoeing around sone that night in the tunnels. I was so lost in it, that I grabbed her hand. "Do this for us." Her eyes widened and she started breathing funny. I could feel her palms get sweaty from my touch. My heart quickened at the thought of me pinning her against the car door and kissing her so good that even she wouldn't be able to resist the urge to let me have my way with her in the backseat of that car of hers.

"I don't know." She tucked her hair behind her ear with her free hand. I backed her into the car door, consumed with a fierce passion that I knew was possibly showing. I placed that soft hand on my chest and slipped my other behind her head. Her eyes were caught in a trance by my luring gaze.

"I can't. She quickly turned around and hopped into the car and drove off as if the place were crumbling down behind her. I kicked a rock nearby, hating myself for letting her slip through my fingers like that.

I was no longer play innocent. The lord knew that I was struggling with that shy boy bull crap. Things needed to happen faster and judging from her reaction to just me holding her hand alone, having her would be a cakewalk.

To make matters worse, my phone went off and my self-hatred was now channeled to the stupid girl who couldn't read between the damn lines.

Maybe if I had sex with her, I could relieve some of this pent-up hellfire that I'd been harboring. One thing that she hated more than anything was a man whore, and I was going to give her the biggest man whore she'd ever seen.

I answered the phone. " What the hell have you been up to? I have been trying to call you all week." The stress was just eating her alive and I couldn't help but feel annoyed as hell.

"I was busy moving. What are your plans for tonight?"

"I'm at your place right now. Mindy and I are hitting it off quite nicely."

That was enough to make my blood run cold. There was no way in hell I was going to be able to pull off a one-nighter with that one. She was psycho as hell.

"You went to my house without my permission!" I had to remain calm or my whole life might get destroyed.

"It's not like I haven't been to your house before." She sounded hurt.

"That was when my family wasn't around." My jaw clenched as words came out.

"She wants me to have dinner with you guys. Come home soon. She made kissing noises and hung up the phone.

When I drove up to the house, I had to fight the urge to ram my car into the back of hers. I dropped my backpack at the door once I was inside. I could smell spices in the air and hear female laughter. I walked into that kitchen and found her putting lettuce in taco shells. There was an entire platter Mindy was topping them off with a layer of salsa.

"Oh, hello Ares. I hope you're in the mood for something that will set those taste buds of yours on fire." She glided her hands over the Platter as if they were magic.

" I shared the family recipe with her." Megan licked some salsa off her finger, in a way that made me so damn uncomfortable, I had to stay strong. That day she was wearing a tight black dress that sparkled and her eyes were thick with liner and those irresistible lips were coated with plum. I had to calm myself down before this went south quickly.

"I'm not hungry." I swallowed hard.

She walked over to me with her chest poked out and pressed it against my chest. I wasn't going to lie, I was dying inside, as my manhood expressed how excited it was to see her psycho ass. " You always used to eat my tacos." She poked out her bottom lip and walked her fingers up my chest. I gently placed my arms on her shoulders, sweating profusely, and stepped back. Now that she was at arm's length, I could gather my thoughts.

"We need to talk." I took her by the hand and dragged her outside. I slammed the door behind me as well. She caught me off guard and flung herself at me, grabbing all on me as those lips overpowered mine. It took all the willpower I possessed to get the damn parasite off me.

" I don't want you anymore." She left me no choice.

She rolled her eyes in disbelief and placed a hand on her hip. " Are you sure about that? Back there you seemed to be extremely excited to see me."

"I will always be sexually attracted to you, but I will never give you the one thing that you desire most of all."

"Go tell that to someone who doesn't know you." She captured me by the chin and gave me another unwelcomed kiss. I shoved her back.

"Get the hell out of here now!" Headlights hit the driveway and my dad pulled up to the house. When he stepped out of the car, he looked as shocked as I'd been when she told me that she was at our new place.

"Megan!" He shouted on the way over. " What a pleasant surprise. I should have known that you would be back in town with the Area's crazy behavior." He hugged her and kissed her cheek. Now I was stuck with her for dinner.

I sat through torment, hating every single word that escaped that mouth of hers. I literally pictured myself ramming my fork through her damn neck and watching blood spray all over Mindy's face. It would serve her right for letting a crazy bitch into our home.

When I finished my plate, all I gathered from there, what seemed like an endless conversation, was Ares has some of them still in. I think they are in his room." That snapped me back to reality.

"Sorry. What?" I cleared my throat.

"Those old records that your mom used to love. You don't listen to them anymore and so I'm sure that it would be alright if you let Megan borrow them for her grandma. Just for a little while." I directed my attention back on the demon who had gloating eyes as she took a victorious drink from her blue glass.

" When I find them, I will give you a call."

"They're in your bookshelf." Mindy just had to chime in. She rose from the table and encouraged me to take Megan to retrieve them and walk her to her car after we found them. Then she cleared away our plates and started washing them up in the sink. Megan walked over to me and latched onto my arm, smelling like lavender and dragging me up from my seat. I could have broken her damn neck right where she stood if I had nothing to lose, but there were too many witnesses and I had bigger plans.

When we reached my room, I grabbed the four records that my mother cherished with all of her heart. She snaked her arms around my waist before I could face her. Instead of seduction, she sobbed into my back.

"You love me. I... know you do. Please let us go back to the way things were." I pried her coiled arms from around me and thrust the damn records into her hands before she could strike again. I no longer felt sympathy when I looked into her eyes.

"I will walk you out the door." I had to shove her down the stairs a little, to end my misery sooner.

Chapter Eight

Samora

I sat there waiting for the phone to go off. My father called from downstairs. I found him in front of the television with a bowl of popcorn, watching a horror flick. He almost sprang from his seat when I joined him. I couldn't help but laugh.

"You almost gave me a heart attack." He held onto his chest looking as if he'd seen a ghost.

"Hey, you called me down here." I folded my arms.

"I need you to be completely honest with me right now."

Oh, great. That's never a good sign. What can you possibly want to discuss with me now? It'd better not be about boys.

"Have you been sleeping with that boy?"

My heart froze and then discomfort spread through my entire body like wildfire. "I haven't even seen him beyond school but twice and you think I'm sleeping with him? I hate how you won't just let the past go."

"I'm only asking because when I went to call his parents the other day, an old woman picked up the phone. If he's staying with her until they get back, then she is someone who can be easily manipulated. That's why I asked."

I wrinkled my nose. " I would never do something like that with an old woman in the other room. Who the heck do you think I am?" I was so over that stupid conversation and stepped out onto the back patio, to debrief and unwind by the pool.

That day the air was cool and there were a few cloud remnants in the blue sky. The sun was out, but not overwhelmingly scorching the earth. I took a seat on the blue beach chair in between the white and purple one and closed my eyes, silently praying for Ares to call me. The wait was weakening my wall of patience defenses and infecting its soldiers with anxiety.

I was nearly passed out when I received the text message from him. My heart leaped for joy when I opened it.

Ares: You ready for some fun?

Samora: Heck yes!

Ares: ready when you are.

I sprang up from my chair and ran inside. My father already permitted me to spend the night with Arianna, so If I got too drunk, I could just crash at her place. That was If I made it out the door.

I scooped up my gym bag next to the front door. "Be safe." Sounded more of a threat than a warning with his stern facial expression. With that being said, I pulled my bag strap over my shoulder and was out the door.

When I reached Ares' place, there wasn't a car in sight. I shot out a text you Arianna to see if she would be heading over soon. I didn't. Get a response. Then I sent one to Erik. He had been really nice to me lately and surely; he would keep the conversation flowing throughout the night. I didn't want to drink so much that I forgot where the hell I was or made a fool of myself. A text was sent two minutes after I sent mine out

Erik: I will be there shortly.

At least the odds were somewhat in my favor. I hoped to God that Arianna would show up to even out the female species. Being drunk with two guys was a terrifying thought.

I waited an extra four minutes before entering, to give the others some time to show up. When that fell through, I hopped out of the car and rang the doorbell once I got on the porch. Ares answered the door after the third ring.

That night he was wearing a blue collared shirt with a huge skull in front with cursive letters in what may have been Latin. His hair was damp, and he smelled like I imagined someone to smell like after a cologne commercial.

"You look nice." He grinned.

I was wearing a black blouse with a frilly V-neck with some grey shorts that had slits down the thigh and a few strings hanging from the bottom of each pant leg and through some of the holes in the leg. I wore some heels to increase my height by a few inches. My hair was straightened, and my bangs were side swept across the right portion of my forehead.

I thanked him with blushing cheeks and said that he looked fairly good himself. That made me die a bit on the inside because it sounded cheesy to me.

Hello, regret five million.

He led me into the living room. The place had black leather couches intersecting the television. They had an oval-shaped coffee table in front of the long couch that had a basket with their remotes in it. On either side of it were two candle holders with spiral-shaped, black candles. The back wall was covered with family photos. In each corner stood an onyx lion that was about five feet tall. The scent of the room was floral.

He told me to make myself at home while he went to fetch us some drinks. It looked like I would be using booze as a crutch for a conversation starter after all. He returned with two large bottles of Jack. Then disappeared into the kitchen once more with a bowl of chips and a stack of red cups. While he poured the drinks, I sent out another text to Erik and asked when we should expect him to arrive. He didn't respond that time. My nerves were killing me.

He handed over my cup and took it to the vacant spot next to me. We clanked cups and it was bottoms up. I was thankful to have eaten before showing up. He poured us another and I reached for the chips. We clanked cups once more and then downed the next cup.

"I wonder what's with everyone today." I skipped tipsy land the drunk wave wiped me out.

"What do you mean?" He took a chip out from the bag and started crunching away.

"How are we supposed to have kick back with only two people?" I took another chip and set it on my tongue and started chewing. The barbeque flavor hit the spot.

"What? You think they're going to flake on us?" He poured another cup and took a drink.

"You know what?" I poked him in the cheek. " Forget about them." I laughed. He placed his arm over the back of the couch.

Suddenly the front door opened and a man who assumed was his father stepped through the door. Judging from the look on his face, he was just as surprised. His father's eyebrows pulled together as they ping-ponged back and forth between us.

"What the hell is this!" Ares shot up from the couch and marched over to him with his fists balled up and his jaw clenched. "You think you can do whatever you want? I told you no company tonight!"

"Why must you ruin everything and make me the damn bad guy all the time!"

His father wrinkled his nose. "That doesn't smell like beer!" My heart was jumping each time one of them shouted.

I rose from the couch. "I think I should go."

"Drive her home! As soon as you get back, the two of us are going to have a long talk." His father shouted after us when we were on our way out the door.

Before he helped me into the car, he pressed me against the car door and kissed me so passionately that my head was spinning long after he released me. Then opened the car door for me. I was so confused. I had him drop me off at Arianna's place. He lingered in her driveway until I was safely inside. The door was unlocked when I got there. I didn't question it and just walked inside.

I found her watching television on her stomach, holding onto a pillow with her back legs in the air, crossed. I stood there in the doorway with my arms folded and the wrath of Satan in my eyes. I cleared my throat to let her know that I was present. She jumped.

"You scared the crap out of me!" She gasped and motioned for me to take a seat.

"What the hell was that back there! You said that you would come and then you just ditched me." I could feel the waterworks coming on. "It was a disaster."

"He told us not to come." She said in their defense.

"What? No. He was worried when he thought you guys weren't coming." I took a seat at the foot of her bed with my legs hanging off the edge.

"He must be one hell of an actor." She pulled out her phone and showed me a text message from him.

Ares: don't bother showing up. I just want to spend some one-on-one time with Samora. I can tell that she and I are attracted to each other and I feel like you guys would be a distraction. Don't get mad. You're the best. It was forwarded to Erik as well.

So, the debate began. That was extremely sweet of him to want to be alone with me. Then there was the fact that he lied to me about it. Was he going to be just like the others? I couldn't have that, but he was so darn cute. I had some serious thinking to do before I got too carried away. I had to thank God that his father came home unexpectedly. It gave me time to figure things out. The last thing I needed was more drama. Especially after my last boyfriend.

I sent Ares a text asking if everything was alright before going to bed that night. I had to make sure that I didn't complicate things further with his dad and he didn't complicate things with mine.

Ares: He's pissed for now, but he will get over it. I don't think it should stop us from seeing each other though.

Samora: I think that we should cool it for a while. You know just until we are in a better place.

Ares: Is that what you want?

My heart sank to the pit of my stomach. I was already a little more attached after seeing him and his father feuding. I needed to breathe a little bit.

Samora: It's not what I want but I know that it will benefit us in the long run.

I didn't get a response after that. I tossed and turned the rest of the night until sleep overpowered me. The next day, I felt empty inside. The entire day was a huge buzzkill. I had a terrible hangover and threw up four times before I could hold anything down then when everything was good again, I ended up with a killer migraine and then stayed in bed.

"Arianna! There's a boy here for you!" I was surprised that she dared to have a boy over when I was suffering.

When she was gone, I didn't know what to do with myself. I felt uncomfortable in my own skin. My mind was consumed by the horrible memories of my dead relationship that I no longer cherished anymore. Besides the sex. Now those memories I would probably need an exorcist to deal rid me of them. I needed some fresh air and fast. I snuck out the back door while Mindy and my father were chatting away about whatever. I found myself parked out in the alley of Samora's house. The curtains were open, and I could make out her brushing that gorgeous hair before bed. That was one lucky brush to be so damn close. I could just imagine the heat radiating off her skin with each stroke. I sat there on the hood of my car, trying to imagine what her room looked like.

She was artsy and abstract, so maybe she had a painting, Starry Night by Vincent Vangoh above her bed. She loved rock and metal, so there could have been posters on the other walls of her favorite bands. She always smelled so delicious. I could just see a bordered-up, black vanity with nothing but perfume and body spray.

I then pictured myself draped across her bed watching her climb into bed over top of me. That was enough to bring me back to my natural state of mind. I wondered could she feel how much I desired her. This was far beyond attraction. Was she thinking of me now? That made the corner of my mouth rise. She had me addicted.

When my eyes began to grow heavy, it saddened me to leave. I found myself driving back home, feeling incomplete. I got home and dropped down on the laid face down and then turned my head to the side to turn off my lamp.

I went to sleep and found myself lying on a black beach under thick cloud cover. The waves were massive and crashing violently. Lightning struck in the distance and thunder cracked like a whip. When I lowered my eyes, a shovel appeared in my hands along with a freshly dug hole to fit my size. Suddenly the skies split open, and the head of a scythe broke through and fell out of the sky. I woke up before it made contact. I was drenched in sweat, gasping for air.

Chapter Nine

Ares

I was beyond mad. If Mindy hadn't shown up that night, I would have killed my father. When I was done with him, the glass coffee table was shattered to pieces and all of its contents were mixed up in the shards. The television that I cracked over his back, the screen was jacked up so bad there was no way that it was cutting on ever again. I used the rope in an attempt to strangle him with it when she stepped through the door. She had to pull me off before he was past the point of no return. I slept in my car that night and booked a hotel room for the weekend. Since the love of my life wanted to take things slow, I was going to seize the opportunity to catch up on much-needed rest and recuperation time. It wasn't easy but when I realized that I could just check on her by using email, that eased my tormented mind. I was apart from her but not completely and to me, that was better than nothing.

The poor girl was suffering from a mad hangover, so I had Arianna drop off some hangover snacks and drinks. She sent me a text message thanking me so much for it later on that day. I was so happy to hear from her that I didn't know what to do with myself.

That Monday, I found her in the parking lot with the last person that I wanted to deal with or expected to see again. " Hey, Megan. What are you doing here?"

"I told you that I would be coming back to school." She was dressed in a pink frilly blouse with a miniskirt. She had a case of lust eye.

"I just wasn't expecting to see you this soon," I spoke through clenched teeth.

"I was just catching up with Samora. Apparently, you were lost without me." She walked over and grabbed me by the cheek. "But don't worry. I'm not going anywhere ever again." I broke away from her at the sound of the bell and grabbed Samora by the arm to let the psycho know that I was already spoken for. I could just imagine all the hateful thoughts rushing through her mind at the time.

Maybe that would also make Samora jealous enough to stake her claim on me already. Lord knew I was dying to ask. I needed to make sure that we were both on the same damn page. One minute she was shoving her tongue down my throat then the next she was shy as hell. I knew that alcohol played a key role in two of those kisses, but damn. I wanted her to say that I was hers and tell Megan to piss the hell off.

During ceramics, I managed to twist up two strands of clay that were wide at the bottom and thin at the top. I cut off the access and attach it to the head. Once that was secure, I moved onto the neck and torso. I would stop just below the breast area and start working on the other details. While I was working on it, Samora asked me how things were back at home.

"I told you before not to worry about it."

"Are you... never mind." She guarded her eyes and went back to her project.

"What?"

" Are you and Megan going to get back together?" Spewed out of her mouth, causing me to slice through the wrong part of the flattened clay that I had out.

"What makes you think that?" I stopped everything I was doing to pay attention to her.

" The way she was speaking to you today. I know that the two of you have a history and if you really want to be with her then you should. She is far more comfortable with you and you guys know more about each other."

My heart went into panic attack mode. "If I didn't know any better, I would think you're trying to get rid of me." I gave her a nervous laugh.

Her eyes widened. "I know what it's like to have loved someone once. It isn't something that goes away overnight. She even told me that she came back for you. I don't want to hinder you from being happy." She sighed.

"That's not what I want at all. I thought you picked up on that after we kissed like three times and went out on a date for crying out loud."

Her cheeks turned red. I could feel my own heating up after I said it.

At lunch, Erik was the one to bring Megan over to our table. She quickly stole the empty seat next to me before he could. Then Erik stole the empty spot next to Samora before Arianna could take a seat. Arianna was livid, grabbed him by the back of his collar, and forced him to take the one next to Megan. Everyone was howling with laughter at that one.

"I was thinking that we should all go to the movies this weekend."

I shot that one down fast." We have already been this month. There is nothing else that is cool enough to watch. Besides, I'm grounded."

"What'd you do this time?" She groaned

"None of your business." I opened my plastic container of salad and drizzled ranch over the lettuce leaves. I picked up the egg in the corner and tossed that bad boy into the lid portion of the container. One thing I hated most of all in the food department was a freaking boiled egg.

"Why are you so moody today?" Erik asked.

I was so annoyed that I bent my plastic fork. Samora was kind enough to sacrifice hers. I felt like a freaking jerk for taking it. She had a burrito with some dirty rice and fruit salad. She wasn't going to enjoy them because of me.

"I'm annoyed. Megan why the hell are you here? Don't you have your own friends?"

"I do but I thought that you guys would be cool to hang out with. That's all." She looked extremely hurt, but there was nothing that I could do about it. The damn girl mistook my kindness for being back in business with her and that was not happening ever again.

" Really? Is that all?" I scoffed.

"I don't know what is going on with you, but I think that you should channel all that negative energy into something more productive." The seduction in her tone of voice was sickening. If I wanted that then I would just have to unleash the beast within when I was alone with Samora and that would be the end of that. The only reason why I had been settling was that I wanted to make sure that she loved me with the same amount of passion as I did for her. How could I when She was questioning my feelings for that psycho bitch?

"How about after school we go do something?" Erik asked her.

"You know what? That sounds like fun." She gave him the flirty grin that she used to use on me a long time ago. She thought that by agreeing to go off with that piece of human garbage she would bring out my jealousy. Too bad there was none left.

After lunch, the rest of the day was a huge bore. I made it through the rest of the day without any homework, so all that was left was to video chat Samora. I hated being apart from her like this. Why did she have to be so close, yet so distant? Before she picked up, I stripped out of my shirt and tossed it across the room. It landed in front of my closet on the floor. She eventually picked up. Her cheeks were beyond red.

"I thought since you and I couldn't see each other for a while that I would video call you." She got a laugh out of that one. "Just when you thought you'd shaken me for good." I winked at her.

"What happened to your shirt?" That made the corner of my mouth raise.
That meant that she was thinking about how irresistible my body was.

I scratched the back of my head and let loose a yawn, I used it as an excuse to give her a good view of my awesome body. She looked as if she might dic of hcat stroke as she watched. "I was hot. Sue me." I laughed.

"You are such a mystery to me." She smiled, tucking her bangs behind her ear.

"How so?" I cocked a brow.

"Well, one minute you're guarded and the next you're open. You wouldn't by any chance have a case of bipolar disorder, would you?" She teased.

"I am in a constant struggle trying to figure out what type of guy you want. You are a very shy girl, and I don't want to go on hot too soon or I might never get the opportunity to show you that I'm not only after your body."

Please set the beast free. Please! He has been dying to ravish you, so bad. I need this! Once you've had him, there is no going back.

"I'm sorry if I gave you the impression that I am non-status, but there are some things in my past that I don't like to revisit. I can't allow myself to be off my guard or it will happen again and the last thing I want is to be looked down on by others. My father especially."

"So, he caught you with someone?" She started fidgeting with the string of her hoodie and from the looks of its shame.
I didn't want her to ever feel like she couldn't come to me with anything. The lord knew that I was the last person to judge her.

"Some things are better left in the past, buried close to earth's core to turn into ash where they are no longer existent." Damn, that was almost poetic. She was so deep at times.

"I'm not here to judge you. I just want you to be more open with me that's all. I want you to figure you out so bad." I was feeling extremely exposed as if my man card had been stolen from me. Right in front of her face. She had that twinkle in her eye again and that to me was like a million fireworks setting off simultaneously inside of me.

"How about we start over then?" She leaned her hand on her cheek.

Please don't say back to point A again.

"Take me out on a date."

Now that I can do it. it

"Where do you want me to take you. The sky's the limit."

"How about we have a picnic. The atmosphere will be peaceful and not that fancy. If you want me to open up to you then I need to be comfortable."

Who knew Samora could be so demanding. It was kind of a turn-on.

"And what shall we eat on this date?" I grabbed a pen and paper from my desk and brought them back to bed with me.

She tapped her finger on her top lip, thinking with a flirtatious smile that drove me insane. "How about we dine on ribs, mashed potatoes, and for dessert chocolate cake?" I jotted everything down and said done.

"Not quite." I was baffled. "I want you to bring us a bottle of grape soda."
I scribbled that down.

"And a bottle of wine," I added curtly. " Gotcha." I did the wink snap at the computer screen.

" The only thing to do now is to settle on a date. When did you think we should get this romantic date going?"

"How about we try for next week?"

"Alright." I scribbled that down.

There was a knock at my door. "I've got to go. Goodnight." I slammed the laptop shut when Mindy entered the room.

"There are some things that we need to discuss. I made dinner. Could you join me please?" She stepped aside and followed me out the door and downstairs to the kitchen.

Her kitchen had grey, black and white backsplash with black countertops and white cabinets. The fridge was silver with the fridge in the bottom that pulled out like a drawer. She had a photo of her and my father's trip to Carlsbad Caverns stuck to the fridge with a Paris magnet. Black curtains were hanging over the window above the sink. She had a silver toaster with a matching blender. The table was an oval-shaped marble surface and black legs the chairs had oval-shaped backs with white cushions. The smell of pot roast filled the air. There were only two bowls of it set out on the table.

"Is dad not joining us tonight?" I took a seat across the table from her.

"He felt that I would be better suited to discuss what is to be done about your behavior."

"My behavior!" I pointed at myself and scoffed.

"Now calm down." She looked as if she was on the brink of having a damn heart attack.

"Pray tell what he is planning on doing about it." My nostrils were flared with my arms folded.

"He feels as if you need to go to therapy." She sounded as if I were going to jump over the table and strangle her or something. I wished that I could, but what good would that freaking do?

"I'm not going to therapy." I shoved her damn pot roast away from me.

"It's either that... or you're getting kicked out."

Chapter Ten

Samora

I didn't know if I was ready to open up to him about my past just yet. I didn't know how dominant the deceptive part of him was. For him to manipulate me like that just wasn't going to slide with me. I had to make damn well sure that he wasn't going to hurt me. When Juan and I split up, it shattered my entire world, broke me down to the core, and lit me on fire. When someone's world is stripped from them, they don't trust easily.

He sent me a text message, asking if I was ready for our date. I scanned myself from head to toe. That day I was dressed in a purple dress that flared out at the bottom, along with some matching sandals that laced up the calves. My hair was in beach waves and I had a black, glossy bow clip on the side of my head.

I sent him a text saying that I was ready, as I made my way downstairs. He sent me a winking face and I met him out front. My father was out for the afternoon and wouldn't be back until later that night, so it provided the perfect opportunity to go out with him.

He had some soft rock playing on his stereo when I got in. He had on a grey button-up shirt with a pair of skinny Jeans and smelled like a rich man. His eyes lingered on me for a good while, looking pleased with what he saw. My heart started fluttering.

When we reached the park there was not a soul in sight. Our park was infested with trees and had a huge pond with a bridge over it. There were a few picnic benches scattered about, along with two jungle gyms. One for the smaller kids and the other for the older ones. There were a gentle breeze and a few remnants of clouds spread across the blue sky.

We walked around the back of his car and pulled out a plaid picnic blanket and handed it to me while he took the picnic basket into his free hand and closed the trunk. We found a spot beneath the biggest tree in the park. He set down the picnic basket and I helped him open it up on the grass. I could hear the sound of geese flying overhead and see a few bugs buzzing and hovering over the ground nearby. This was truly paradise.

He grabbed the picnic basket and pulled out some Tupperware which contained the ribs, mashed potatoes, and chocolate cake. He opened the large one with the ribs first and held it up to my nose. A smile spread across his face as I took in their hickory aroma. It was mouthwatering.

"Did you cook them yourself?" He got out the plastic plates and silverware.

"No, I actually had a good friend of mine cook them for me." At least he was honest. "Are you disappointed?" He asked with those vulnerable eyes.

"Not at all." I smiled, as he handed me a plate of ribs and potatoes.

"Good because you're the first girl that I have ever taken out on a picnic before." That warmed my heart a little more than I was expecting.

Keep it together woman! This guy is slick as hell and the last thing that you want to do is get too tangled up in his charm.

I instantly regretted ribs when I started struggling with the damn fork and the thick juicy meat. " Here. Let me help you out." I felt so damn childish. He literally peeled off one of the ribs and held it up. "Go ahead." A devilish grin spread across his face. I scrunched up the corner of my mouth and shook my head no. "Oh, come on." He baited me with those puppy dog eyes. I would feel worse if I left him hanging, so despite myself, I took a bite from it. He set down the rib. " You've got a little something." He threw me off guard and literally licked the corner of my mouth with his eyes focused on my mouth after. I sat there paralyzed with a heart that was banging against my ribs to the point where I thought it would burst through them.

Arianna was going to have a field day when I tell her about this.

He was the first person to break free from the trance to winch we both found ourselves in. I adverted eye contact and tried out the mashed potatoes while he worked on his ribs. The potatoes had just the right number of garlic and butter to produce the most appetizing flavor.

"So, tell me something about yourself that I don't already know." He sucked barbeque from his thumb.

"Well, I'm not much of a party person." He didn't seem surprised.

"It shows." He laughed.

"I suffered a huge breakup that I had a hard time recovering from. That's why I held off dating for the longest time."

"You used to date that Juan guy who moved. Right?" I nodded.

"I absolutely despise having to explain myself more than once."

"What was that again?" He teased. I couldn't help but laugh. It was refreshing to see him so relaxed. The guy was always extremely serious and tense.

"What are your biggest fears?" He brought out a thermos of chilled wine and poured it into red plastic cups. He handed a cup to me and I took a drink. I was going to go easy on the booze for the day. I didn't want my dad to find out He wouldn't let me live to see another day.

"So that you can use them against me? No freaking way." I peeled off the meat from the bone with fingers coated in thick barbeque and took a bite. I was being smart about it this round.

"I will tell you mine." He offered.

"Okay. I'll bite." I set down my ribs and before I could lick my fingers, he took my finger and suctioned it off, sending a surge of electricity throughout my entire body. That wicked grin returned before he took another drink of his wine.

This guy was going to be a freaking handful. My mom always told me to beware of the silent ones. They were silent because they were always scheming. There was no way in hell he was ever setting foot in my bedroom.

"I have a fear of heights and a fear of death." He shoveled some mashed potatoes onto his fork and took a bite.

"Mine is being abandoned and snakes."
The word snake had a double meaning to it. I drank some more.

"How about tarantulas?" He laid down on his side, using his hand and arm to support his head, looking like a dreamy male model. My body temperature skyrocketed.

"Not a fan." I laughed. That cooled me a little.

"If I were a tarantula would you still be interested in me?"

What kind of question was that?

"I don't know. I guess that would have to depend on how nice your web was." I instantly regretted saying that one. That was another thing about myself that I couldn't stand and that was when things I said came off as perverted when I had no intentions of it being that way. Judging from that corner of that gorgeous mouth rising and the glint of amusement in his eye, that was exactly what happened.

"Some say that it's spectacular." Even his laugh was flirtatious. I hated my life so damn much sometimes.

"That is not what I meant." I frowned. " I was trying to be crafty. He laughed.

"I was only teasing you." He sat up and opened the container that had the chocolate cake in it. Then took a fork and offered it to me.

"What is with you today?"

His brow was cocked with the corner of his mouth raised. "You said that we were starting over, so why not take a different approach?" He offered once more; my cheeks almost caught fire when I took a bite. "What do you think?" It practically melted on my tongue.

"Please tell me you made this." I laughed.

"I did." He took a bite himself. His eyes closed and his smile widened. Then he handed me a fork and we both dug in.

When we were finished eating, I helped him stow the picnic blanket and basket into the trunk of the car then we took a walk around the pond. I had so much fun with him that it saddened me when it was time for us to part ways. When I stepped out of the car, he walked around to my side, captured me by the arm, and spun me around to face him.

"We should do this more often." He grinned.

"I would really like that." His gaze lowered to my mouth and his face drew closer and closer to mine. I forgot how to breathe. When he nuzzled his lip between mine it sent off an electric current of ecstasy throughout my entire body. After our lips parted neither of us could stop smiling.

"I'll text you tonight." He said, breathlessly.

"Alright. I will be looking forward to it." I pulled away from him and we said our goodbyes. I got inside, into my comfortable clothing, and washed the smeared makeup off my face. Then I turned on the television so that it appeared as if I had been lounging around all day.

Dad came home three hours after my return. He went straight to my room and gave the door a knock. "Come in!"

"Samora I wanted to apologize to you for overreacting when I found out about you and that boy."

I knew there had to be a catch somewhere. "I want you to be open with me from now on. We don't have the best track record in the communication department, and I don't want things to carry on like this. You are a teenage girl and a responsible one at that. I know that you won't disappoint me. Bring him by so we can all get acquainted with one another."

There it was, little did I know that there was going to be far more surprises down the road for us at dinner.

Chapter Eleven

Ares

I found myself sitting across the table from the old scumbag. That black eye made the corner of my mouth rise. Served him right for embarrassing me in front of Samora. When I kicked his ass that day, I kept imagining how shitty she must have felt when he barged in unannounced.

"So, have you considered my offer?" He had his arms folded and his brows pulled together.

"I would rather live on the streets than spend another second with you and Mindy."

"I'll bet you would just love that. Too bad. You're getting therapy and that's final. I can't have you roaming about as if your actions don't have consequences. Do you want to be a dead-beat father? That's what will happen if you piss your future away. No son of mine is going to be human waste."

He was so lucky that we were in a restaurant or I would have beat him to death right there. The waitress came back with my iced tea and his sandwich.

As soon as she left, I said to hell with that. "You think I'm going to listen to the man whore who drove my mother to suicide?" He looked as if his head might explode, his face was fiery red and the vein in the left portion of his forehead looked as if it might break through the skin. His brows were knitted together then in two seconds his body tensed up and his eyes bulged. The next thing I knew he fell to the floor clutching his chest.

I got out of my seat and started crying for help. The next thing I knew I was at the hospital with Mindy soaking my t-shirt with her tears and the doctor explaining to me that my father had a heart attack. The lucky bastard didn't die, so that was good news. His downfall was my gain. I could use this to get closer to Samora. I sent her a text message as soon as we hit the parking lot.

She sent her condolences. I told her not to worry too much and that he was just going to have to take it easy for a while. The following day was a Monday, and I couldn't have been more excited to get that damn sculpture completed. The sooner, the better.

I didn't bump into Samora until later that morning when school had begun. I was in the process of removing my work from the locker when I looked to my left and found her taking out her clay. When our eyes met, she blushed and smiled. I smiled back and winked at her.

When I got back to my seat, I worked on the swan necklace. I wanted to make it a heart-shaped cameo with the swan in the center and made to resemble lace. I used a reference picture to get the ball rolling. While I did so, she asked me how my father was doing. I looked her deep in the eyes. "I'm still a bit shaken up over everything. He is still in the same condition that he was in when he was admitted. I hope to God that he makes it through all this." Remorse infected those gorgeous, brown eyes and I couldn't help but smile on the inside.

He was due back home in two days. They wanted to keep an eye on his heart rhythm and make sure that he wasn't going to encounter any more complications in the meantime.

"You poor thing. How about I treat you to lunch today?"

She wanted to buy me lunch. How considerate of her. I loved how compassionate she was. No doubt in my mind that I hook line and sinker this one.

When lunchtime came around, we were on our way to the parking lot when Erik made his unwelcomed appearance. He snaked his way between us and draped his arms over our shoulders. "Where are we eating today?"

I removed his arm from my shoulder. "We aren't going anywhere. Samora and I are going to lunch as a couple. You can go bother someone else."

Did the moron completely forget that he and I were supposed to be on the opposite side of the fence?

Just my luck, when we reached the damn restaurant, Arianna, Megan, and he was seated at the vacant table near ours. "Ooh!" Arianna's eyes widened. "Are the two of you on a romantic date?" She shook her brows up and down, giving Samora a nudge in the arm. Megan looked as if she might attack Samora at any moment.

"Why do you have to be such a buzz kill?" I asked and she stuck her tongue out at me. Samora was more bashful than ever.

"I think we should pull our table together. There is no way in hell they can genuinely enjoy romance with the pressure of all of us present." With that being said, the jackass literally joined our tables together. Megan was stuck right beside me. Occasionally I had to slap her hand away from my leg and lean away when she tried to press her arm to mine. Don't even get me started on how I had to endure her poking her breasts out in my peripheral vision.

"So, what brought the two of you together?" Envy was just radiating off of Megan's skin.

"It was when I smashed his pottery in Mr. Gold's class. We kicked each other's ass, and she was more than willing to help clean up the mess I made."

She gasped. "Why would you do something like that?"

"Have you met him? The guy is a total jerk. He has no freaking morals or even a soul for that matter." Arianna fake smiled at him. His expression was unreadable.

Could it have been that the two of them were secretly hooking up behind everyone's back? If that kept Erik occupied and far away from Samora then that was fine with me. If he dared make this a love triangle situation, he would find himself leaving in a damn body bag. He just had better not have been using Arianna to get to Samora. Then I would do more than kill him. I would chain him up to a tree, hack him up with a chainsaw, blend his carnage into a blender and then force Megan to choke on it.

I sent Samora a text under the table, asking if she would be free that afternoon. She pulled out her phone from her purse and told me that she had to take care of some things and then she would be completely free. I invited her back to my place by just sending her my address. I told her that it would be a surprise location. Mindy was going to be gone for the afternoon and that meant we would have the house to ourselves. My father really couldn't have picked a better time to have a heart attack. It was scoring me major perks with her.

When she arrived at the house, she called me when she reached the front porch. I only knew because she told me she was on the front porch. "Are you pranking me right now?"

"I'm kind of hurt that you didn't remember the address." I teased and let her inside."

"Well, you didn't exactly label the place, my house." She laughed and hung up the phone. I tucked mine into my jacket pocket. It was another one of those cloudy days and the air was a bit chilly.

"Would you please step inside." I took a bow. She walked inside and called me a cheese ball.

"You already have a cute nickname for me?" I awed.

" Oh, hush." I stopped her when she was about to turn toward the couch. She raised a brow looking up at me.

A devious grin spread across my face. "You and I are going to my room." I grabbed her by the arm and tugged her along.

"Don't get any ideas." She warned.

"Who me?" I said in a teasing tone of voice.

"I'm serious." She did sound serious, but she would be whistling to a different tune once she was comfortable on my nice bed.

When we reached the room, I pulled out my old stereo from the closet, set it down on the corner of my desk, and put on some soft rock. She walked around the room taking in everything. A smile spread across her face when she spotted some of the abstract posters hanging by the closet. I didn't have them hanging in the other place because I didn't want my walls cluttered, but since I knew she was going to be in my room, I thought it would impress her.

The piece that she had her eye on was one of myself sitting in a bloody bathtub with my fingers weaved together and my elbows pressed to the sides of the tub. I had a bloody smile and razor-sharp teeth. On the wall behind my head was a pair of eyes with blood pouring down the backsplash.

"This is really nice. When did you make this one?"

I folded my arms, trying to think. " The fifth grade." She smiled and said that it was wicked awesome.

"Thank you for thinking so. I am far more advanced now, but I'm glad that you can appreciate it."

I took her by the hand and guided her over to my bed. She looked a little hesitant at first then she complied. "So, was it all that you'd imagined it to be like?" I propped my cheek on my hand, laying on my side.

"I thought that you would have some of your ceramic pieces on a special shelf or something."

"Sorry to disappoint you, but I don't keep the. Ceramic things I make because if I did, I would spend all day critiquing the damn things and it would drive me insane." She looked at me intrigued.

"What do you do with them then?"

I have a secret place I bury them out in the woods. I call it the masterpiece cemetery. One day in the future someone will unearth them and find a note that I stuck in the hollowed-out bottom of each one with my bio on a piece of notebook paper." Her eyes widened.

"You truly are one crafty person." She smiled with a twinkle in her eye.

"Glad someone thinks so."

"Are you hungry?"

"Starving." She blushed.

I climbed off the bed and extended a handout to her. She crawled over to my side of the bed and used my hand to get down. Her palms were a tad sweaty. That put a smile on my face. She still wanted me.

When I got downstairs, I grabbed some leftover lasagna from the night before and the spatula from the drawer next to the sink and carved her out a square and myself. I popped those bad boys into the microwave one at a time, watching the plate spin and heat up.

Oooh that mouthwatering cheesy layer.

After we ate dinner, I took her out on the patio, where I got to sit as close as possible to her and take in that peach-scented body spray of hers. I weaved my fingers through hers. She looked down at our hands, both of us were smiling like fools.

She leaned her head back with her eyes closed soaking up the sunshine. My eyes trailed down her neck and lingered on her breasts. She was definitely a sight to see. I would probably dehydrate and starve to death watching her sit there.

Time went by too fast. When she left, I felt like a piece of me had died. I locked myself up in my room and cranked the music loud, trying to cope. Eventually, I drifted off to sleep.

Chapter Twelve

Samora

I was headed out to the parking lot for lunch when I was stopped in my tracks by Erik. He asked me if I was busy.

"No. Why?" I folded my arms.

"Just wanted to know if you could hang out with me for the afternoon. Don't worry. I won't keep you long. There is just a girl that has been trying to hook up with me and I want her to know that I'm not available."

"Then why don't you just tell her that? She will know that I'm not with you when she sees me with Ares."

"She's in college. There is no chance of your paths ever crossing again."

"I don't know. It's a small town." I gnawed the inside of my cheek while waiting for him to give up.

"I thought you and I were friends? This girl goes to the university and that's located in the town over." He encouraged.

"Fine, but you will have to make sure Ares doesn't see. I can tell that he's definitely the jealous type. Oh, and you owe me food."

He winked and snap-pointed at me.
"You've got yourself a deal." I wanted to make sure that Ares didn't see us leaving together, so I waited for Erik to leave the parking lot first.

He messaged me saying to follow him over to the mall. I would be nice and make him Grab me something from the food court. They had these amazing chilly cheese fries that I always found myself buying when I took trips with Arianna down to the mall. I liked to have myself a milkshake with it to eliminate heartburn.

I parked my car a few cars down from his when we got to the mall parking lot. After I stepped out of the car, he draped a damn over my shoulder unexpectedly. I got away from him.
"I want her to think it's legit." He enclosed the distance between us and placed his arm back over my shoulder. "She could be watching us right now."

He opened the entrance door for me, and we took a seat at one of the benches. He sent out a text to the mystery girl and we waited for a response. She didn't take long. "Let's head over to the arcade."

Was she for real?

I hadn't been in that part of the mall since I was twelve.

As soon as we walked in a redhead with green eyes and a tiny gap on the side of her smile walked overlooking confused and hurt. She was petite and had a black beanie, cut-off shorts, a blue tank top, and converse.

"I thought you would be coming along." She folded her arms sizing me up with a potent case of the judge eyes.

"This is my girlfriend, Samora." That stupid arm was placed around me once again. She scrutinized both of us and then sighed.

"Well, we'd better get over to the cinema. The movie will be starting at any moment. I only bought two tickets, so you will have to buy your own."

"I'll pay for her." Squeezed me.

The entire walk over, I caught her eyeing us with disappointment. When we reached the concession counter, he paid for popcorn and some milk balls. For drinks, he ordered me a Pepsi and himself a coke. The movie that we went to see just had to be a romantic comedy. It was about a girl who fell for a guy who lies about being a lawyer. It was called My lovely Imposter.

I munched on my popcorn in peace until the bastard placed his stupid arm over me. I hated how close he was sitting he smelled as if he stepped out of a cologne factory. I could feel eyes on me. When I looked up, the poor girl's nostrils were flared. I hoped to God that she wasn't going to be the type to fight. That would just be my luck though. If it resorted to something like that, I wasn't sure if I would be able to take her. Size didn't matter.

I'd only been in one fight my entire life. I was in the sixth grade and a girl was talking crap about my other friends and I ran my mouth. The next thing I knew she shoved me, and I had to use a purse to defend myself. When all was said and done, she tried to play the victim by saying I hit her five times. For some strange reason, neither of us was punished too badly. We had to do a week of community service. That girl was tiny too, but she was strong. If it hadn't had been for that purse, It wouldn't have ended the same.

Erik caught her glowering and then he had to overstep and weave our fingers together and lay his stupid head on my shoulder. I sat there paralyzed.

By the end of this stupid date, you are going to try and give me more than dinner? Be prepared to be disappointed, you, psycho man. I can tell that you are enjoying this way too much.

After sitting an hour and forty-five minutes of pure hell, she took off without so much as a goodbye. Erik walked me to my car.

"Now that's over, be prepared to be my slave for a week."
He held my door open for me with an eyebrow cocked.

"I thought that you just wanted me to take you out for
dinner?"

"No. I wanted for you to pay for me to enjoy a meal. I
never agreed to go anywhere with you. You put your arm
around me, laid your head on my shoulder and you even
held hands with me! Not to mention the fact that she stared
at me with murderous eyes throughout our time together." I
got into my car and strapped myself in.

His brows pulled together with a smile on his face. "I think
you are protesting way too much. Could it be possible that
you have feelings for me?"

"Get over yourself." I scoffed and jerked my car door
closed, laughing at how ridiculous he was. He was far from
anything that I would ever date. I liked mystery men with
edge and wore a ton of black. I could care less about pretty
boys that were so full of themselves that they couldn't see
anything past their own reflection.

I reached the house and my father sat there brooding. He
shot up out of his chair and marched over to me, with hell
burning in his eyes. " Where was your young lady?" His
nostrils were flaring like a dragon breathing fire. And his
face was extremely red.

"I had to help Arianna with a project for school." I tried to look him directly in the eye, but my eyes were starting to pool.

"That's funny because I just got off the phone with her and she was at home and she said that she hadn't seen you since you guys had class together."

I was caught.

" I am going to ask you one more time. This time I want the truth." He tapped his foot with his arms folded and the skin between his brows scrunched up, looking like a sideway sandwich. " I know that you were with that boy again. Hand me your phone now!"

I grudgingly handed the phone over and he sifted through my messages and since Ares was the only boy that I had in my contacts that I messaged a lot, he called the number then to make things worse his stepmother answered phone instead of him. My knees were knocking against each other and sweat slid down the side of my face. By the time he was off the phone with her, I had some explaining to do to Ares and the worst dinner of the century.

He handed me back my phone. " I'm so disappointed with you. Why can't you get yourself a boy that wants you to achieve a high school diploma? I will be damned if I let you try to drop out of school again. You lost so much already. Thank God they let you make up for the twenty-six days you lost that summer, or you would be flipping beacon at the Breakfast shack." He dismissed me to get my homework done.

Chapter Thirteen

Ares

I stepped out of the shower and toweled off and wrapped the towel around my waist. When I stepped out into the hall, Mindy was waiting for me with displeasure all over her face.

"What's wrong now?" I groaned.

" When are you going to behave? Is it not bidding enough that your father is in the hospital recovering from going into cardiac arrest? You only have a few more months before school is out and you're screwing around with some poor girl."

Where was all this coming from?

"Yeah, her father is furious about you encouraging her to stay out, rather than going straight home today."

Now I was really confused. I didn't do anything with her today.

"You know what? If you land yourself in jail, don't expect us to bail you out!" She stormed off.

I went to my room and called Samora. She didn't answer the phone. I needed to know who took her out. I sent her a text and told her to call me back. She sent me a text message and explained everything in a paragraph. I tossed my phone across the room after I read the damn thing. How could she be so stupid? Erik was going to die. He couldn't just let me be happy. He had to taint everyone who loved me. I paced the room with my fists balled up at my sides, trying to keep calm. I couldn't wipe the image of him being that close to her out of my head along with torturous flashbacks of him and Megan's sucking face.

Did he find the smell of her peach body spray irresistible? Did he imagine her naked every time he saw her? Did he literally think that I was going to let him steal her from me? Was Megan not enough! I hated his guts so damn bad; I could strangle him! I quickly got myself dressed. There was going to be hell to pay, and I wouldn't be satisfied until his blood was on my knuckles!

I parked my car outside of his house and beat the steering wheel with my jaw clenched and sweat making its way down the side of my face. I was trying my best to hinder myself from committing murder but the thought of that jerk all over my girlfriend was not something that I could let slide. I marched up to his front porch and beat my fists against the door until his father answered the door.

"Oh, hey. Haven't seen you in a while. What can I do for you?"

" Is Erik home by any chance?" I couldn't stop moving. My fists wouldn't be satisfied until they bashed that man in his whore face. She was mine! All mine and he needed to know that I was the only one that she would be going home with! Me!

"Is everything alright? You look upset." He adjusted his glasses.

Get a grip. Get a damn grip!

I forced a smile. "My aunt just died, and I could really use a friend right now." I bit down on my bottom lip so that my eyes could water. The taste of blood pooled in my mouth and my eyes did the job.

"He isn't home right now. If you want me to tell him that you stopped by, I will."

That would have to do for now. His date with the angel of death had been postponed for now. I decided to blow off some steam back at home on. some videogames. Every victim that was slaughtered brutally in my head they had Erik's stupid face. Once I got it all out of my system, I snuck downstairs and raided my father's liquor cabinet. After emptying the bottle, I found myself texting the asshole some threats. About an hour later I found myself hunched over a toilet seat that I stained with my chunks. When sleep found me, I couldn't tell you when. I woke up on the cold tile with a pulsating head and someone banging on the front door. I used the side of the counter to get to my feet and dragged myself down what seemed like an endless flight of stairs until I answered the door.
Suddenly Erik charged right at me knocking me straight into the glass table that contained two vases and a wicker

bowl that held our keys. The vases were smashed into a million pieces. I grabbed him by the collar of his shirt and head-butted him. The impact of our heads colliding somehow relieved my head throbbing pain.

Before he could do anything else, I need him right in the staff sending him falling back onto the floor. I got up from the table as he got to his feet, I caught his fist in my hand before it contacted my face.

" What the heck is wrong with you!"

" You are what's wrong with me! You took my girlfriend out on a date!"

He jerked his fist out of my palm.

"It wasn't a real date." He hunched over. Trying to catch his breath as he held onto his knees.

" That's no excuse! You don't screw with another guy's girl! It was really freaking cliche of you to try to sink your venom into my girl! Do you know how many dumbass movies they have where this shit goes down? You think I am going to let you take her from me! I think not. I will put you in a body bag before I let that happen. You stay the heck away from her or I will slit your freaking throat!" My blood was boiling, and it was taking a ton of my willpower not to bash his skull in.

"Dude you need to chill the hell out. I don't want your damn leftovers. You and I both know that I would never betray you like that."

He was full of crap if he thought I believed that for a second. Or on meth! Wouldn't put it past him.

His phone rang and that was the end of it for now. We were far from done. I wouldn't be satisfied until I had a knife stained with his blood in my hands. She was mine and I would be damned if I let him take her from me.

He hung up the phone." Hey, I have somewhere I need to be. I will catch up with you later."
Just as he turned away, I captured him by the arm. " You have better respect my wishes. You know what happened to the last guy that double-crossed me." Seeing the fear in his eyes and his sudden gulp made my dark soul smile with satisfaction. He quickly broke away from me nearly stumbling over my shoes by the door on the way out. Mindy popped in after him looking as if she'd just witnessed a murder as her eyes met the broken vases on the floor. Out of no freaking where she struck me across the face. It stung for quite some time after. I tried to rub the pain out as she gave me the scolding of the century.
" What the heck is the matter with you! Those were from my mother. I know that you don't have respect for human life but the least you can do is respect the dead. I will never get those back." For a second I almost took pity on her but then I remembered being knocked into it by a prick and that wiped that away.
" Hey, I was attacked. I'm not a freaking monster. If you want someone to blame, blame the jerk that tried to steal my girlfriend and slammed me into the stupid table in the first place." I left her standing there angry texting Erik.

I was in desperate need of a shower. I reeked like a sweaty brewery. When that scolding hot water touched my skin it was like heaven on earth and sobered the heck out of me. When I stepped out of that shower, I smelled like a cologne model.

Chapter Fourteen

Samora

Arianna sat at the edge of her bed with eyes the size of Saturn. " You did what? Oh my gosh! Did Ares find out about it! When did Erik start having feelings for you?" She started spouting questions a mile a second. I plopped down in her desk chair threw my head back unleashing a groan as I spun it around to face her.

" listen Erik and I aren't nor will we ever be a thing. Ares is amazing and everything minus a few quirks that I ever wanted in a guy. I'm not sure if he knows but I hope that he never does. I really have a complicated situation on my hands back at home too. My parents found out that I wasn't studying with you and I just can't catch a damn break."

"It's like you're in a freaking soap opera. I totally think that Erik is really into you. Especially after all those juicy details. Out of curiosity, are you certain that there is no spark whatsoever?"

I sprang up from the chair and left her standing at the top of the staircase asking more ridiculous questions.

Speaking of the devil I got a text from Erik. He apologized to me for overstepping and then he just had to take it to the next level of ridiculousness. He asked me if he could make it up to me over a slice of pizza.

Samora: I don't think I'm ready to forgive you yet.
Erik: Don't be like that. You know that at some portion of that fake date you were actually having a blast with me.

Was he being serious? I would have rather been dipped in acid and my bones ground into dust than experience that date all over again.

Samora: Look I don't think Ares would approve of you making moves on me. Maybe you should focus your attention on someone that appreciates you and doesn't want to be with someone else.

Erik: I asked you to go out for pizza. I didn't ask you to be my girlfriend.

Finally, I struck a nerve. For a moment there I thought that nothing I could do would tick him off.

Samora: I don't trust you and therefore I would never go anywhere alone with you ever again.

Erik: Fine! Be like that. I thought that you and I could have been best friends but since you feel that way, I guess this is goodbye.

I sat there in Arianna's driveway in shock. I must have read it three times before I responded. This was far too easy. There had to be a catch somewhere.

Samora: Is this a joke?

Erik: I'm dead serious.

Samora: I didn't think that you would give up so easily. I'm surprised.

Erik: I only go all-in when there's something to fight for.

Ouch! That one stung a little.

Samora: Okay then. Good luck with your future conquests.

Erik: I would say the same, but I don't give a damn. Bye.

Wow! That was unbelievably easier than I thought it would be. Yay! No love triangles in my soap opera. So awesome.

I stuck the key in the ignition and backed out of that driveway listening to my favorite song on the entire planet. For once a situation that I encountered had been easily solved.

My phone went off again later that afternoon this time Ares was the man of the hour. I sucked in a deep breath and picked up the phone.

" Hey." He cleared his throat.

" How's it going?" I started gnawing my inner cheek.

" I was just thinking about you and wanted to see how you were." His voice truly sounded concerned.

" I'm a little grounded but other than that I'm fine."
He let out a sigh of relief. " Thank God. "

"Did someone say something to alarm you?

There was a slight pause before he spoke again. " No! Not at all. I just worry about you when you aren't near me. That's all." My cheeks struck fire and my heart began to flutter.

" You still there?"

"Y-yeah."

" Before I let you go. I just wanted to tell you that I don't think that it's a great idea for you to hang out with Erik. He has a real dark side and a girl like you shouldn't get entangled into that mess."
My blood ran cold. Who told him about the fake date with Erik! I could already foresee a blood bath in the courtyard

at school. Just when I thought there was nothing else that could possibly complicate my life, there it was like a damn slap to the face.

"You don't have to worry about Erik. We are from two different worlds with nothing in common."

" That's good to hear." I thought I would have heard some released tension from his voice after I assured him, but that didn't happen.

"I've got some things to take care of. I will see you at school." He hung up. I buried my face in my pillow and screamed a few times before tossing and turning the remainder of the night. I fell asleep at two in the stupid morning feeling even more tired than before I passed out.

I dragged myself out of bed and grabbed the first two items that I spotted in my closet. Which was a black lacy blouse along with a pair of dark skinny jeans. Then headed to the bathroom and took a quick shower to wake me up. Then I headed downstairs and brewed some coffee and poured it into a coffee cup and bolted out the door.

Once I reached the school my stomach became queasy as I got a flashback of the last conversation that I had with Ares. I didn't want to run into him but at the same time, I didn't want him to get expelled for fighting with Erik. I pulled out my phone and asked Erik if he had seen Ares without fully thinking about the last conversation that I had with him. Of course, he didn't reply.

" Darn it!" I snatched up my belongings and made my way to the art building.

" Hopefully he is in there beating clay instead of bashing heads in."
My heart stopped when I didn't find him there. I pulled out my phone texting him and saying a silent prayer as I did.
A few minutes later my phone went off.
I picked up as quickly as I could. "Hey. You on campus yet?"

" No, I had to get to a doctor's appointment I should be back around second period. Make sure Erik keeps his paws off my work."

" I thought that you said you wanted me to steer clear of him?"

" Watch from afar." In the background, I heard a nurse call his name. He told me goodbye before hanging up. I could finally breathe again. The bell rang and. I spotted Erik holding hands with the last person I ever expected him to hold hands with.

" Arianna!"

What the heck was she thinking? The bastard even planted a kiss on her cheek. On the way into the classroom. *This had to be a freaking nightmare*! I pinched myself a few times as I made my way to my seat. I never broke out of it. This was clearly not a bad dream. It was my worst freaking nightmare come to life!

I couldn't focus on my work for crap that day. They were glued together at the hip. I knew that this was going to piss Ares off, but I had to fix this before things got worse for me. I caught Erik at lunch on his phone by the boiler room. He had this stupid grin on his face that made me sick to my stomach. I knew who he was texting and waiting for. I quickly grabbed him by the collar of his stupid plaid shirt and dragged him over to the back of the gym which was only a few feet away as he shot a crapload load of questions.

" What gives?"

I folded my arms. " What the heck is going on with you and Arianna!"
He planted both hands on my shoulders with a smug look on his face." Don't worry about it." Then he strolled off. I was hot on his heels.

" Oh I, am worried about it. If you hurt my friend, I will murder you!"
Arianna waved at him from the boiler room with a raised brow. He quickly ran to her and scooped her up in his arms like in the freaking movies and they were on their way to the cafeteria.

Ares just pulled into the parking lot. "Samora!" He called out. That was just not my day.

" So, what did I miss?" He placed an arm over my shoulder.

" You have no freaking idea."

I took him to the cafeteria without thinking. When he saw Erik making out with Arianna it was like looking into the face of pure evil. He dragged me over there.

They pulled away from each other and Erik didn't seem in the least bit phased by his presence. He poked his straw into the carton of his milk and sipped it away casually.

" What the heck is this? Are you trying to die early? This is pathetic even for you!" Ares said through a clenched jaw.

Erik put his milk down and rose from his chair. "Are you my mother now? You should know that even she can't stop me from doing whatever the heck I want. Arianna and I hooked up last night. He winked in her direction her cheeks turned beet red and she tucked her hair behind her ear.

"Whatever the heck you two have brewing isn't going to work because Samora is mine!" To hear those words come out of his mouth made a heatwave wash over me to the point where I had to get the heck away from them all. I heard Arianna call out to me. The next thing I knew she was walking beside me.

" You are walking way too fast. Where are you going?"

"You all are losing your freaking minds and I can't take all this crap! I only got a few hours of sleep last night. I didn't even eat breakfast yet." As I reached the parking lot a swarm of jocks and cheerleaders rushed in the opposite direction of us and that was when I knew the fight was on.

" I know that you're pissed off and confused right now but Erik really is the hottest guy I have ever been with. We aren't dating or anything just friends with benefits. I am not looking for something deep right now. I just want some fun."

" Fight! Fight! Fight!" The chants grew louder and louder. We were now the only ones not watching the fight of the century.

At the end of the day, they both got expelled for fighting. Ares had a busted lip and a black eye. Erik however was hospitalized with a broken nose cracked rib and a missing tooth. I was surprised they didn't press charges after that bloody massacre.

Chapter Fifteen

Ares

Seeing my father in that hospital bed was enough to make anyone cry. Samora was going to me for dear life as if her own father were in that bed. I had to admit it gave me a strong sense of power and was hot as hell. Mindy was away at work, so she didn't have time to kill the vibes. However, that didn't stop the devil's daughter from making an entrance.

"Megan!" Samora and I shouted in unison.

She was dressed in a black dress that had a low collar and hugged her curves in all the right places. Her round shades were perched on the top of her head and she had what looked like nine-inch spiked heels on. She strolled in with a bouquet of roses and a get-well card.

"I don't care about what happened between us. Your father will always be my family."

Samora backed away from me and dried her eyes. The next thing I knew her phone went off and she was leaving us.

" What? I don't even get a goodbye?" That was one of the worst feelings ever. She apologized then hugged me before disappearing. I didn't understand why when things became a little shaky it sent her running for the hills. I really was dying to have her witness me beat Erik to a pulp. If I could redo it all over again I so would. Just to see how she would react. She came back to me, so I knew that my other side had to already have had a foot in the door.

Megan walked over with her arms folded. " So, you guys have finally reached that place in your relationship."

"Want to elaborate?"

"The whole meeting the parent's thing. Now that I think of it, can you actually count this one? I mean, after all, he is unconscious. I also remember having to break into your old house just to get an introduction. That makes me so curious about your current relationship because every time I enter a room you forget to breathe." She nibbled on the end of her fake nail in a way that made me hot under the collar. I backed away.

"You aren't my judge."

"It's okay to admit that she is a rebound. I am pretty hard to get over. Just last week Erik couldn't get enough of me." She stepped forward backing me into the wall.

"Show some respect for your elders." I shoved her back blinded by the flashbacks of Erik with his groping hands all over her.

She started laughing. "Now there's the Ares I know. By the way, there were fresh flowers placed on Dion's grave today." She blew me a kiss and walked off like she owned the place.

Something had to be done about Megan before Samora found out about Dion. I can't believe that I totally forget the anniversary of the guy's death. His case was still cold which was great for us, but the guilt kicked in once more just when I thought I had finally escaped my past, leave it up to Megan to conjure it back up again. I didn't understand why I had to be the one to feel guilty. He was the monster, not me.

I said goodbye to my dad, snapped a photo to prove to Mindy that I had actually been there to visit, and left the room. On my way down the hall, curiosity got the best of me and I just has to check out my handy work. I had to stop myself from laughing at the sight of his cast and bandage-infested body. I couldn't help but wonder what man whose blood tasted like. If he weren't under surveillance, I would have taste-tested some.

"Sleep well, Erik." I slid my hand slowly down the glass taking in the smudging sound before I left. Served him right for trying to steal what was mine. I wasn't going to be so easy going with this one. As soon as I laid eyes on Samora I imagined him coming for her and I was ready to finish him off if this bull crap continued. Dion wouldn't be lonely anymore and that would be a win for him. It would be the least I could do after the wretched life he inflicted on us all. Erik always wanted to be his favorite and who would I be to not grant him the privilege.

When I got home that night, Mindy was waiting for me with salad and pasta. There was a catch to it when she asked me to get the silverware. I pulled an application for therapy.

I crumpled it in my fist and tossed the forks down before going to bed that night. She sent me a text two minutes after I logged into my email account.

Mindy: You aren't getting out of this one.

I tossed my phone and went to bed. when I woke up Mindy ordered me to sign the wrinkled application. I pulled out a lighter from my top drawer. Her eyes out up thinking that I was going to pull out a pen but instead I took out my trusty lighter and torched them in front of her face. She snatched them out of my hand and extinguished them with the glass of water on my nightstand which had been there for a few weeks. The room now reeked of burnt paper and when that alarm went off, I took a stretch.

"I don't think it would be appropriate Mindy if you stayed and watched me dress." She didn't even speak. Hell was all over her face and she marched right out and slammed the door.

I knew that I couldn't hold her off forever the next day my father would be coming home. He would have been home sooner if it weren't for that overly cautious doctor of his. The man literally was thrown into Florentine for a chest cold.

I thought I would dress to impress that day. I pulled out a black button-up satin shirt with a collar and a pair of matching slacks with silver skulls on the left pant leg. I also grabbed my massive skull belt and put on my spiked collar. I looked slick as hell. The last thing I slid into was a pair of studded leather boots with a crap ton of buckles down the front.

When I arrived on campus, there were some winks whistles along with a few car horns. I felt like the man of the hour and nothing could stop me from having the best damn day of my life.

I hit pottery class early just to get ahead. That day we were making coil pots. I got to kneading the clay and all that jazz then shaping it into three-dimensional skulls when the bell rang.

Arianna was the second to enter. She looked at me as if I were the devil himself as she approached me. "You really had no right to pummel Erik like that." I rolled my eyes and carried on with my work.
"I don't see how Samora could stomach being anywhere near such a monster." I couldn't help but laugh my laugh wasn't adding up with it.

"She has good taste. You on the other hand not so much. If you only knew how many girls that guy pulls in a week, you wouldn't be standing here having this pointless conversation with me. Megan was not only my Achilles heel, but she was his too. At the end of the day, he will always be at the end of her hook because he desires everything that I have. Right now, he thinks he can get under both Samora and my skin so that he can be the king for once but what he can't stand is when someone doesn't instantly fall under his charm. If you're easy he will get bored with you and peruse that which he cannot have even more. Just a little something to ponder while you wait for your precious boy toy to recover." Samora stepped into the room when Arianna took off in an even pisser mood than before. I could care less. She wanted to be in that pit and so she would stay, get heartbroken and lose her best friend.

"What was all that about?"

" You can't expect her to be thrilled to see me after I placed Erik in the hospital."

She placed her bag on the desk before breaking out the new lump of clay that she would be working on and the materials. I was done with the first two layers of the pot and continued the process until the bell rang. There wasn't really much to talk about with her. I honestly hoped that she would complement how sleek I looked that day, it killed the badass vibes for the day. I avoided her at lunch to make her feel the pain of my absence. I hung out at the pizza joint until the bell rang. The rest of the day was a total blur. She didn't text me until school was out.

Samora: I didn't see you at lunch. Are you alright? I hope that whatever Arianna said didn't get to you.

Ares: you don't have to worry about me. I just like to be alone some days. Did you miss me?

Samora: What do you think?

Ares: You should come to keep me company tonight.

Samora: I don't think your stepmom would approve of an unexpected guest.

It was time to bring out the big guns. I stood up and snapped a few photos. One with a puppy dog expression biting down on my lower lip. Then the second one I gave her a wink. There was a pause after I sent them. I wasn't in the least bit alarmed because she was taking in all my glorious body.

Ares: Is it convenient enough for you and me to have an adult sleepover?
I couldn't help but grin.

There was no response, and since I was bored out of my mind, I paid her an unexpected visit of my own. I just was dying to break in and roll around in her bedsheets naked. She had her eyes glued to her phone for sure. The look of desire possessed her eyes. It was such a glorious sight to behold. I stayed out there watching her until her lights cut off.

The next day there was a huge ruckus going on downstairs. My grandma's raspy voice sliced through the silence and almost made my heart explode. I grabbed my navy-blue housecoat that hung from the inside of my closet, meeting with her downstairs. The last time I came down in just boxers she asked my dad if he allowed me to become a porn star.

When she saw me thus tine, she thruster her tan suitcase at me and told me to bring it to the guest room before following Mindy into the kitchen with the list of items she could and could not eat.

After dropping it off I sent Samora a text good morning.

Samora: Good morning.

Ares: I will be seeing you tomorrow, I hope.

It would be Sunday and I knew that with my grandma aground I would be busy catering to her and my father that day.

After entering the kitchen grandma gave me a slobbery kiss on the cheek that reeked of peaches and salami. She squeezed my cheeks and looked me over. " Is it just me or do you look more handsome than the last time?" She laughed.

I shrugged and pulled away from her. " So, have you come to see dad?"

" I was really just stopping by on my way to the mall, but I thought I would be considered heartless for not paying the old fast a visit." Mindy shook her head with distaste.

It was around two in the afternoon when we got the call to scoop him up from the hospital. Grandma had a list of chores and errands for me to run as suspected. By the time she left Mindy and I was down for the count.

We sat on the couch with our necks draped over the back of the couch. " Remind me to take a few shots and drink a couple of energy drinks before she shows up the next time." She slapped me on the leg breathlessly and retired for the night.

Chapter Sixteen

Samora

Flashback:

I sat there holding the pregnancy test in my hand at the airport feeling overwhelmed by the future that awaited Juan and me. The Dion waited patiently outside for me to come out with the news. Sure, enough I   found myself staring at a red positive symbol. My heart was on the brink of an explosion.

What the heck am I doing? I have no job. I hope to God that Dion's dad comes through or we won't even have a roof over our heads. How are we even going to survive without obtaining new identities? The police would just drag us back home and this trip would have been for nothing.

Outside the door, could hear bickering. Quickly the bathroom door swung open, and my father snatched the pregnancy test from me. "Get your stuff. We are going home." I had never felt such a whirlwind of emotions in my life. I protested. He dragged me kicking and screaming out of the bathroom. Ethan tried to fight him off, but security was called and the next thing I knew, I found myself soaking my pillow messaging Juan why he didn't show up to the damn airport that night.

I placed the photo of us back into the shoebox which contained all of our love notes, tiny plushies, jewelry, pregnancy test, and photos we took together. I slid it back under the bed and dried my eyes. My heart still felt like a pit sometimes and there would always be something to trigger those unbearable emotions. Today was the anniversary of our separation.

I knew I shouldn't have but it was worth a shot anyway. I pulled out my phone and texted his number. Apart from me wanted his number to have changed. Then the other wanted desperately to see if he was okay. Sure, enough I got a text message back.

Juan: Hey Samora bear.

A teardrop streamed down my face. The hole in my chest only seemed to get deeper. I couldn't breathe.

Samora: You still have my number?

Juan: I know, pathetic right?

Samora: How are you?

Juan: My brother just got out of rehab. My mom is trying to bail my grandpa out of jail again. I'm fine for the most part. Got to stay strong for the family or we will all be screwed. Lol

Juan: How about you?

Samora: Erik started sleeping with Arianna. Megan and Ares came back to school. I guess things could be worse.

Juan: Wow! Arianna and Erik. That's insane. You would think that Ares and Erik would have been killing each other over Megan.

I sat there for a moment feeling extremely awkward and out of place.
So much had changed over a short course of time. This was a mistake.

Samora: I've got to go. My dad wants me to take care of some chores.

Juan: Alright Samora bear. Text me anytime.

I quickly got off the phone and deleted the messages. I went into my contacts and my finger hesitated over the delete icon where his number had been highlighted. I sucked in a deep breath as my index finger drew closer. Then I just found myself shutting the damn phone off and had a good cry until I drifted off to sleep.

The following day Ares texted me to see if I would be ready to hang out the following day. His dad would be coming home today, and his grandma would be visiting. There was no way in freaking hell I was going anywhere near that house. Meeting the family was sort of like a

'We're engaged!' Thing. He hasn't even officially asked me to be his girlfriend yet.

I dragged myself out of bed and my phone went off once more. This time it was Arianna.

Arianna: We need to talk.

Samora: Alright.

Arianna: Meet me at the Tasty Yogurt in an hour.

Samora: Sounds good. See you then.

When I showed up, she was sitting near the window with her eyes glued to her phone screen. She looked so down in the dumps I took a seat across from her.

" Oh good. You're here." She called over a waiter and ordered the frozen yogurt with strawberry chunks. I ordered the same.

" What did you want to talk about?"

She put her phone away, weaved her fingers together, and perched her chin on them. "You and Ares need to respect our free will. You are in a relationship and need to focus on your issues. Did you know that yesterday was the day you and he that shall not be named broke up?"

I shifted uncomfortably in my seat.

"Judging from that look on your face you went to sob fest town when it hit again. So, would you tell Ares to keep his fists to himself until I get bored of Erik?" The waitress returned with our yogurt.

"Ares has a mind of his own. I had nothing to do with the fight." I stuck my plastic spoon into my yogurt and took the first bite that sent my taste buds on a trip to enjoyment land.

" Just out of curiosity have you ever considered showing him a good time. You know like... In bed?"

I started choking like crazy. "What the heck!"

"Maybe you could take his savage nature by giving him a treat." She threw up her hands. " That's all I'm saying."

"What makes you think that I would sleep with anybody after you know who? My father flipped crap on me the last time that I just sat there at his place. If I got caught with Ares, I think he would literally kill me."

"Has he shown that kind of interest in you?" So many silent offers came flooding back to my mind. I got all mushy just thinking about it, but I snapped out of it quickly before it showed.

" I will take your silence for a strong yes. It's time for you to move on. I'll bet Juan has already been with half the girls in his new town. I just want to see you happy, and I want to be temporarily happy with my Erik! Is that so much to ask for!" She slammed down her fist on the surface of the table causing me mad anxiety.

" I'm not sleeping with anyone. What happens between Ares and Erik is none of my concern." I took another bite of the delicious chunk of strawberry heaven.

" What of Aires doesn't get as lucky as the other times he's fought with him and he's the one on the gurney?"

"Fine! I will reason with him for your sake but there is no way I'm sleeping with anyone until I graduate." With that being said we enjoyed our yogurt and parted ways.

Chapter Seventeen

Ares

Flashback:

I sat there on the floor, rocking back and forth, trembling uncontrollably. As I couldn't pry my eyes off the bloody battered corpse that laid before me. Dion dropped the crowbar and dragged me to my feet. "We have to leave now!"
With that being said, I followed him out the door and we stayed up all night driving. My mind kept flashing back and forth between the blood bath and the battered corpse. My heart nearly exploded when my phone went off in my pocket. All the color drained from Dion's smug face. " Don't answer it!" He threatened. I pulled the phone out of my pocket and saw that it was a call from Erik. When I didn't answer, he left me a text saying to meet him at his mom's lake house. When I told Dion, he parked the car near the outskirts of town where there was a red barrel on the side of the road before entering the forest. There we tossed in our clothes and changed into the ones that he had in a duffle bag in the trunk. We factory reset our phones and met with Erik at the lake house, where we stayed the rest of the weekend. For a while, I was being tormented by Dion's stepfather's ghost. Night after night I would have only nightmares.

I stood in the cemetery hating Dion for putting me through all that hell. I reached into my jacket and pulled out a cigarette. In the distant, sky I could hear thunder. Lightning struck a tree a few feet away causing it to collapse, but that didn't stop me from lighting up. Cigarettes were never really my thing. They were always Dion's.

One afternoon when I went over to his house. His stepfather fell off the wagon again. I snuck through his window with Erik just as we always did, and we snuck down the hall to see if we needed to intervene. Sure, enough we found Dion gagged and tied to a chair as his stepfather burned the poor guy's legs with a cigarette after the cigarette. If it weren't for Erik and me that night putting that asshole in the hospital Dion would have been in worse shape.

I put the cigarette out on his tombstone as raindrops began to sprinkle down. I put on my hood and got back into the car. I cranked up his favorite rock song and headed home for some much-needed booze.

The funny thing about the past is that no matter where you are it always seems to bite you in the ass. He deserved what happened to him. I hoped that he was burning in eternal damnation with no escape for every person whose life he screwed with and took while he was on this earth. Maybe he'll be too docile for him. But what could be worse than that? I gunned the gas to get to my booze salvation. Thinking too much was always one of my flaws it made me feel hopeless.

The next day I arrived an hour late at Samora's house. She when I pulled into the alley. " I'm sorry. I overslept. Yesterday was rough. My dad finally got released and my grandma had too many things for me to do." I held the car door open for her and she didn't say a word the entire time. Her arms were folded, and she kept staring straight ahead.

"You still got in the car. You can't be too mad at me." I gave her a playful nudge.

" I just font understand why I have to cater to everyone else's needs. What about mine? Am I not important! Is it too freaking wrong for me to be selfish every once in a damn while?"

She was not mad at me for sure. I could relax. I sucked in a deep breath and exhaled slowly. Then I reached for her hand. To see those cheeks, turned red was the highlight of my day. I weaved my fingers through hers and smiled. Her face softened and her eyes eventually met mine. " Do you want to talk about it?"

" No!" She tore her hand away from mine.

"Just tell me one thing before we go."

" What?"

" Does it have anything to do with Erik?"

"No." She didn't even look me in the eye. I practically strangled the steering wheel down the road. If the jerk weren't already in the hospital, I would have sent him to the morgue!

I parked the car in a lot of the pizza joint and walked around to open her door. I seized another opportunity to take that soft warm hand into mine on the way inside. Her body seemed less tense after. The corner of my mouth couldn't help but rise.

That day I ordered the spinach mushroom, and she ordered the Canadian bacon with pineapple. We both had iced tea for drinks and chocolate dessert pizza after. I took her for a romantic walk in the park and then caught her off guard on the way back to the car. I captured her lips in mine and pinned her against the car door. When we pulled away from each other both of us couldn't stop smiling. After the date, I lingered in the alley until her lights went off before I headed home that night.

Mindy was waiting for me with a case of a pissed-off face. She had her arms folded with the stupid application for therapy. " We can do this the easy way or the hard way. I get under that you won't like the hard way."

I folded my arms as well. With the words try me written all over my face.

"If you don't comply, I will have no choice but to convince your father to send you to a mental institution."

"You can try." I scoffed on the way upstairs.

" No more games!" She shouted after me. I slammed my bedroom door and cranked up the tunes the rest of the evening. I dozed off.

This time when I went to sleep, I found myself standing with a knife to Dion's throat. He was laughing hysterically and bating me to do it. There was tidal wave after wave of a finger washing over me that just when I almost gave into the beast a loud beeping sound jerked me awake. I was covered in sweat.

Chapter Eighteen

Samora

I was told to meet Ares in the art room before the bell rang but he wasn't the only person that I met up with. Megan was tugging on his skull tie in such a seductive way it made me want to pull an Ares and throw down right there.

"No one understands you as I do. I'll bet she would run away if you unleashed the full you." Struggle was written all over his face. I cleared my throat to make my presence known. They both turned to face me. All the color drained from his face. She snickered and grabbed her purse on the way out.

" What was she talking about?"

He cleared his throat and adjusted his tie. "Nothing." He said curly.

"That didn't sound like nothing." I folded my arms.

"Listen, I already have enough on my plate right now. The last thing I need right now is to fight with you over assumptions."

I couldn't believe he was speaking to me like that. This was not how I imagined our morning. "Why? What's going on with you that's so unbearable?"

"You never tell me about your problems, so why should I?"

"I told you plenty." I was so freaking hurt and shocked.

"The day I asked you about Erik you lied to me Nd withheld information from me. Yeah. I had to hear it all from Arianna herself. To be honest, maybe we wouldn't both be so damn uptight if we just got it done already!"

"Are you being serious right now!"
He enclosed the distance between us getting me all hot and

bothered. It took a ton of willpower to back away from his fresh scented cologne and that irresistible face of his.

"What if I'm not joking?"

I gulped and took a step back. " I don't even know what we are." Was a lame excuse but spewed out of my mouth anyway.

He enclosed the distance between us. I could smell his minty breath as he spoke. " Be my girlfriend." My heart quickened. He wasted no time entangling his fingers through my hair and kissing the heck out of me until my head was spinning and I almost gave into him right then and there, but the odds were in my favor. The bell rang and I quickly took my escape to my locker to get my clay.

He sent me a text on my way back. With a wink emoji at the end.

Ares: This isn't over.

I could barely concentrate the entire class. At lunch, I avoided him like the plague and met up with Arianna in the library. She had a study guide for the next class period, and it was the perfect hiding place. If he texted me, I could always say that my phone had died.

I slammed my bag down on purpose to let her know that I was present and pissed. "Do you know how much trouble your little tantrum got me into today!" I whispered as loud as my lungs would allow and took the seat across from her at the table. She licked the tip of her finger looking unamused and turned the page of her textbook.

" Let me guess, he was on the same page with me. You're freaking out because Juan is still on the brain. I really need to get over that crap already. Thank God that you didn't end up with his baby because he flaked out on you that night anyway. Dion would have been a better father than him. At least he showed up."

"Why must you be so difficult? I don't want to be kicked out of my house because you're scared that he will keep your man candy in the hospital if he thinks that Erik is trying to get with me. Do you know how many times he's hit on me this year? We haven't even been in school that long. You deserve better than that. Besides, I heard a rumor going around that Megan was hooking up with him on and off."

Sadly, I stumbled across that juicy did bit in my math class from a girl named Silvia. Silvia was the student council Queen who knew things that would keep you up at night about people. Her information was always a hundred percent accurate.

"Those are just rumors." She went back to filling out her study guide.

"Courtesy of Silvia."

"You should be thanking me for bringing the two of you closer. Both of you could use it as a chance to blow much-needed steam. He may be even so good that you forget all about Juan."

"I'm so done with this conversation right now." I grabbed my things and hung out in my car until lunch was over.

After school, I quickly made my way to the car without any encounter with Ares. Which seemed far too simple. Just as I pulled into the driveway there he stood, leaned against his car. My heart almost gave out at the sight of him. My father could be coming home any minute!

I just needed time to catch my breath. Was that too much to ask for?

I grudgingly stepped out of the car and he followed me to the porch. As I unlocked the door, I asked him if he'd lost his mind.

"I told you that we needed to talk. I gave you time at school to gather your thoughts. I'm not leaving until you give me an answer." Feeling his hot breath on the back of my neck sent a surge of tingles through my body. I shook the feeling off and opened the door.

I went straight to the kitchen. There was no way in hell I was going to allow him anywhere near my bedroom. I dropped my bag off on the counter, sucked in a deep breath, and turned to face him.

"Ares... Sleeping together isn't going to solve all our issues."

He folded his arms with an adorable, stubborn look on his face. "You didn't answer my question."

"It was more of a demand than a request." It was the best I could use in my defense.

He unfolded his arms and enclosed the distance between us with a smirk on his face. "Be my girlfriend... Please?"

This was the moment of truth. He deserved that much. If I was ever going to move forward in life, then I had to let him in. " Wait right here." On my way upstairs I was beyond shocked that he was behaving himself. I reached under my bed and pulled out the pregnancy test and all of the pain hit me like a ton of bricks.

What the heck was I doing? He would never speak to me again! Why the heck was I self-sabotaging? We could be great together.

Before I could stop myself from revealing it to him, he snatched the pregnant test out of my hand. Tears began to flood his eyes. "Who's the father!" He screamed in my face.

"No one!" I shouted back.

"Let me explain." He threw the pregnancy test at me and started rushing down the stairs. I captured him by the arm just as the front door swung open.
" What is going on here!" My father shouted.

" Get out of my way." Ares threatened in a threatening tone.

My father folded his arms. " Not until you both explain to me what the heck you're doing in my house without my permission."

" I just came to give Samora her phone back. It slipped out of her pocket at school and I just came to return it." He shoved past him and left.

" How did that boy know where we live?"

"Not now dad" I ran upstairs and texted Ares like thirty messages explaining myself. He didn't respond. I hated feeling so useless. I didn't get a wink of sleep the entire night.

Chapter Nineteen

Ares

Flashback:

Dion stood before me in the boy's locker room. Both of us were covered in sweat from running five miles as punishment in P.E for putting Nair in coach James' hair gel bottle. Coach was always a prick to Dion and me for not participating in physical activities. We grew tired of his complaints and since he was obsessed with gelling those golden locks of his, it was payback time.

He slipped on a pair of black plaid shirts while I stuck my head through my grey V-neck. "Not bad for your first day of being off the leash." Dion grinned pulling up his black skinny jeans as I grabbed my shredded ones from the locker.

The corner of my mouth rose. " What next?"

"Well, I was thinking for your reward, I would treat you to a nice distraction. You've been through hell and back and this was just foreplay before you truly break free."

That piqued my interest. " What did you have in mind?" I took a seat on the metal bench and slid into my converse.

"There's this girl I have had my eyes on for quite some time now. She really needs my help. I want her so freaking bad that I just can't... I don't know." He said with a dreamy look in his eye as he leaned his head on the door of his locker. Dion was always the guy that got whatever he wanted and didn't care who he had to eliminate or manipulate to get it. "I need you to take care of something for me. I already did the dirty work. I just need you to send this to his house."

He reached into his jacket pocket and pulled out a thick envelope. No doubt there was cash inside. The address was on the back. In red letters on the front said from a friend.

"What do you mean that you already did the dirty work?" I knew he had a dark side, but I didn't know at the time how dark.

"I didn't kill anyone. If that's where your mind went." He laughed. " Erik and I just roughed someone up and are making sure that the bastard never comes back to town anymore."

With that being said, later that night I went to the address that he sent me to. I parked my car in the alley, hopped over the metal fence in the backyard, and spotted a ladder that was lying on its side against the house. Lucky for me the window was cracked open. I slid it open and climbed in. He should have known that I wouldn't just do something like that without scoping out the territory.

The room was filthy. There was a pile of clothes in the corner of the room. A rock poster on the closet door had a few darts stuck through it. The blue bed comforter was in a ball at the corner of the mattress. A laptop was on with a screen saver of an electric guitar on it. There was a note on his desk that was infested with pocketknives, homework, and rotten food. That explained the terrible garbage odor that filled the air. I picked it up out of curiosity.

Note:

Meet me at the airport. I already got Dion to pay for your plane ticket.

It was in a girl's handwriting. The stupid thing wasn't signed or anything. I thought to myself, how freaking strange. I heard voices coming upstairs and got the heck out of there as fast as I could.

Now it all made sense. It was Samora that he wanted. He was the reason why She never got her closure. He beat the crap out of him and paid him to leave town. I found myself parked outside of Juan's house beating the steering wheel to death.

How the heck was I supposed to rid her of that worthless bastard once and for all? If I killed him that would only make her pine away for him longer. Then it struck me like lightning. I could pay her dad a visit. That would solve it once and for all.

The next day I skipped school and followed her father. To my surprise instead of going to work that morning, I found him meeting up with a redhead at a hotel. This was like taking candy from a baby and really boring. I just wanted to beat the shot out of him just once nit enough to kill him but enough to make him wish that he'd died.

I pulled out my phone and snapped a few pictures before heading back to campus. The thought of Samora worried about me turned me on so freaking bad. Then don't even get me started at the thought of her father's desperate face to keep his dirty little secret. Just willing to do whatever I asked to keep it all a secret. I would milk it for all it was worth.

After Samora left the house the following day, I dropped off a little note of my own for old pimp daddy. Once it was delivered, I was off the school. Things were finally going my way.

Well, that was until the first person that I encountered on campus turned out to be Megan. She linked her arm through mine smelling like jasmine, wearing a tight frilly blouse with a pair of dress pants and high heels. Around her neck was the butterfly necklace that I bought her after our first month anniversary.
What was with girls keeping shut like that? Why not torch it as I did hers on the barbeque grill.

"A little birdy told me that you and what's her face broke up." The false sympathy was sickening.

"I should have known that you would be the first person to come running when I stopped seeing Samora. Then again, you never stopped trying to trap me since you came back to take care of your dear old granny."

"I just thought since you were free things could go back to the way they were"
I removed her arm from mine. "I'm not a dog that returns to its own vomit." I quickened my pace and continued heading to the art building to bash some clay in. I wished that she weren't still holding onto that jerk off. I would have loved to have committed murder. Ooh just thinking about the adrenaline rush gave me a hard-on.

Samora entered the room with her head low and as quiet as the dead. She didn't even try to reach out to me. Arianna pulled me to the side in the courtyard at lunch and gave me a good bitch slap. "What the heck was that for!"

"That was really low of you to not even hear her out."

"She kind of made it clear to me that she was far from over her ex. What was I supposed to do? If she wanted a rebound, she barked up the wrong tree."

" I also couldn't help but notice how friendly you and Megan have been lately. Do you think she's the only one at fault?" I didn't have time for all that unnecessary drama I had a class to get to.

Chapter Twenty

Samora

When Juan left, Dion and Arianna were all I had. My father chose to work extra hours rather than help me get through one of the darkest points in my life. Dion and I would stay on the phone for hours and what I liked about it was the fact that I could discuss anything with him. He and Arianna became my inseparable family. When Dion was murdered, our whole world was turned upside down. It was such a tragedy to die so young. Whoever took him out meant to do it because he had ten-gun shots to the chest. They found his body near a ditch.

Arianna came back to my place after school. I tried my eyes and put on my best casual face I could muster, but just thinking about it only made it ten times harder.

"I talked to that dirtbag of yours."

My heart quickened. "Did he read my messages?"

"Yeah. Unfortunately, he took it all as you using him as a rebound."

"That wasn't what I was trying to do at all. I was going to tell him that day so that he and I could figure it out together. If I were desperate for a rebound, I would have hooked up with Erik a long time ago."

"I really suck at relationship advice. That was always Dion's thing." She frowned.

"I don't know how to fix this at all."

" Maybe you should take this time to stop running away from your grief and let it all go. Then when it's over you can decide if you're ready for another relationship."

That was literally the best relationship advice I heard from her. I just didn't know if I opened that grief door more than a crack if I would ever recover. He never explained to me why he ran away and never came to meet with me at the airport. Maybe that would give me a tad bit of peace.

" I think you may be onto something. I should rip the bandage off. Get ready for depressed me." We both cracked up about that one.

Her phone went off. Her eyes lit up like Christmas lights. That could only mean that Erik was calling. " I' m going to call it a night. Stay strong." She climbed out the window talking to him.

Little did I know that this grief train was only going to accelerate after my dad tapped on my door.

He stepped in looking restless. His hair was sticking up and he had bags under his eyes. " What's wrong?" He took a seat on the edge of my bed and I couldn't help but notice that he was fidgeting with the zipper of his jacket and couldn't meet my gaze. "What's going on?" My heart was on the brink of bursting.

He cleared his throat. " Samora... There's something that I need to tell you. Now I can't live with this secret forever. I... Don't want you to hate me for what I am about to share with you. I just don't think it was fair of me to withhold this sort of thing from you any longer. I have watched you suffer, and I played a huge part in that. I need you to forgive me. It doesn't have to be today. Just when you're ready."

" You're starting to scare me."

"Well, there's nothing to fear. I promise you that. You just have to understand that as a father we can be overprotective of our young and we have a tone more if the ethe experience with life. However sometimes... We interfere and ruin things as well. Remember we're human beings just like you and we don't always see the big picture."

My gosh! I wish that he would just spill it already! My eyes started welling up and I couldn't control it. I had never seen my father cry. This had to be so freaking serious for him to break down like this.

"I have never hated you. You're all I have. I might get mad at you sometimes, but I don't hold grudges. I am one of the luckiest girls in the world to have a dad who not only plays the roles of both parents but cares enough to intercede when I can't see things clearly."

He bit down hard on his lower lip so hard that a trail of blood slivered down his neck. I grabbed a tissue from my nightstand and dried his face. was shaking like a leaf.

" Alright." He exhaled slowly. " The day that I found out about you going to run away with Juan, I hired a teenage boy named Dion to rough him up the day before so that the two of you would never leave together. I had Dion go to the station and pretend to be there to help you, but the reality was I had him there to make sure you never left the airport either."

Just when I thought my heart couldn't possibly take much more. It felt as if someone sawed it in half and I was drowning in my own blood. "You are the reason... He left."

"I understand if you do hate me after all this, but as your father I need you to at least try not to run away again. You're all that I have left as well."

"Please leave." My fists were balled up at my side. I felt so alone with no anchor. No shore to swim to. In a bottomless sea of my own pain and suffering.

The next day at school I decided to finally confront Ares. It would be tough, but deserves face-to-face. All my life I had run from my problems for the fear of losing the ones I loved most. Ho, ever sometimes life provided a mountain that needed to be climbed rather than removed.

I knew he wouldn't answer my calls or texts, so I just went to school and waited for him in ceramics class. He was a creature of habit like that. When he was angry, he would resort to either smashing up clay or someone's face. Since

Erik or my father wasn't around and he would never hit a girl, clay was it.

He entered the room and froze at the door when he looked up from his phone. I stood before him not knowing exactly what to do or say. He turned back towards the door and I captured him by the hand. He tensed up and froze. " I already told Arianna that I am not going to be anyone's rebound." He jerked his hand away. I rushed out in front of him before he could escape.
"Get out of my way!" Tears and anger consumed his faces I'd ever seen before.

"No!" I shouted back in his face. "You need to understand that I didn't start liking you with the intentions of making you my rebound."

"So... You mean to tell me that this whole time I never had a chance with you." His fists were now balled up at his sides and he was speaking through clenched teeth.

"That wasn't what I was saying at all. The pain that I feel for Juan is not the loss of a relationship. It was the pain of why! Why he didn't show up when I needed him the most. All that's left now is the truth that my father paid him off. Then there is the fact that one of my befriend betrayed me. I don't want him back. The reason why I was going to show you my scars was so that you could understand that I wasn't the same person I was before all that crap went down. It takes me a long time to open up and start something new because In all honesty, I don't trust you. I don't trust anyone who shows interest in me because I don't want to be hurt again." Suddenly it felt as if a large boulder had rolled off my shoulders.

"What have I done to cause you any doubts about me?"

I folded my arms. "Let's start with the fact that you and Megan are still attracted to each other. How am I supposed to compete with your first love like that. You lost your mother, and you are violent. Then there was the day that I thought we were all supposed to hang out and I heard from my best friend that you told them all not to come. My father already has trust issues with me as it is. I don't want someone to just use me and run away."

"What a hypocrite. You had a box of your boyfriend's belongings and you still probably message him. The difference between us is the fact that I no longer have feelings for Megan and dealt with them before attempting to have a new relationship with someone else." He shoved past me and left.

Chapter Twenty-One

Samora

I couldn't stop tossing and turning after the most horrid nightmare of my life.

In the dream I found myself standing in a black field that was infested with rotting corpses. The sky was covered in grey clouds. I didn't know where I was running towards, but I felt it in my bones that there had to be some form of an escape from all that darkness. Suddenly I stumbled over a corpse and landed smack dab into a pool of blood. I let out a shriek when I felt a firm grip on my ankle. I tried to free myself but the more I struggled it started to tug harder dragging me closer.

" Why are you running from me!" I heard an all too familiar voice speak to me. When I turned to see his face, I screamed out in horror. It was Juan. I jerked myself awake screaming my head off.

I quickly grabbed my phone and shot him a text. There was no response, so I logged into my email and sent him a message. There was no response. I needed to clear my head. The only thing that I could think of was to take a shower and put on a comedy until I went back to sleep if I were even capable of doing so.

Just as I dried my ringing wet hair, my phone dinged. I grabbed it from the sink counter and was so freaking relieved to see a text message from Juan.

Juan: What's up?

Samora: Just had a nightmare and needed to check on you.

There was a long pause before he replied. So, I sent him another one.

Samora: I know that i shouldn't have contacted you at all, but I was just worried.

Juan: I'm kind of busy right now. Can I text you tomorrow. I'm expecting someone over.

At this hour? Who the heck could he be expecting? Why was I getting jealous? It wasn't like he would stay single forever. Who was I to be pissed? I had been over here trying to start something with Ares when I clearly hadn't healed from the last guy.

If I thought that I was going to get even the slightest wink of sleep that night, I was dead wrong. I sat there with a heavy heart and cluttered mind, as the television played on. My father came downstairs and asked what I was doing up so late.

I rubbed my sore eyes and dried them. He plopped down next to me on the couch. " What's the matter?"

" I just had a nightmare. That's all."

He scratched the back of his head and took a stretch. " You know what helps me sleep at night?"

" What?"

"I go and fix myself a warm glass of milk and take a sleep aid. I don't want you being run down or late tomorrow. Go ahead and go to bed. I will get them for you."

With that being said, I reached my bedroom and shut in my wax warmer for a night light. Then I got into bed. He arrived shortly. It took the sleep aid thirty minutes to kick in.

The next thing I knew my alarm was going off and the sun was beaming down on my face. I slammed down on the snooze button and dragged myself out of bed.

I caught up with Arianna at the front entrance of the library that morning. She greeted me with a warm coffee and a sympathetic smile.

"Thanks." We made our way down the hall.

"Don't worry about Ares. Clearly it was too early to start anything with him. You don't have to be in a relationship until you're ready. "

" Thanks for being understanding."

She placed an arm over my shoulder. " What are friends for?"

When the bell rang, we headed down to the art building. To my surprise, Ares and Megan all chatty before they went their separate ways. She passed by me with a smirk on her face. This was a whole new low for him. He stuck his earbuds in before I could say anything, and he started getting out any air bubbles from his new chunk of clay.

I pulled out my phone and started texting away. I knew that he wouldn't respond but at least he would read the damn thing.

Samora: Hey, it looks like someone calls the kettle black.

He smirked and then turned up the volume on his phone.

At lunch, in the courtyard I found Arianna wrestling with Megan. Both girls had bloody noses. Arianna had a busted lip and frazzled hair. Megan on the other hand was sporting a swollen eye jacked up hair and a gash in her right cheek.

The principal and the soccer coach had to break them up. Ares stood across from me in the crowd with a smirk on his face again. I couldn't believe it.

Both girls were forced to do community service with Janitor Martin during free period, lunch and an hour before school was out.

I texted Arianna when she got home that afternoon. It came as no surprise to me that she was grounded for an entire month.

Arianna: That bimbo had it coming to her.

Samora: Was she worth getting punished for?

Arianna: No one steels my best friend's man like that. Who the heck does she think she is anyway?

Our texting session was interrupted by a call from the very last person that i thought I would ever hear from again.

"Mr. Martinez." I gasped.

"Has Juan stopped by your place by any chance?'

"No, Why?"

" I haven't seen or heard from him for three days ago. I thought he had gotten back to his old self again. Disappearing when we'd fight. Which doesn't make any sense at all. He and I have been on good terms lately."

" The last time I heard from him, he said that he was expecting company. Does he have a new girlfriend or someone that he was going to hang out with?"

"Samora he doesn't have a girlfriend right now."

I felt so freaking relieved to hear it.

" I can try to call him for you."

" Thanks. I don't mind if he is staying with a friend. I just want to make sure that whoever he is that he is alright."

" I understand."

With that being said, I sent him a text message, feeling that it wasn't my place to make a call.

Samora: Where are you? Your dad just called. He just wants to know if you're alright.

There was no response this time. I couldn't stand boys and them waiting like ten minutes to respond while us poor girls sat there going through a rollercoaster of emotions.

Samora: If you could reply sometime today that would be nice.

I needed something to take the edge off. I broke into my secret stash of shooters and downed one. Then tossed the empty bottle into my purse.

I finished up my homework and made my way downstairs for a quick meal. I made myself a tuna wrap and poured myself a glass of soda. It was eating me up inside that he didn't reply to me. I was trying not to come off as clingy.

I called his father back and told him that he didn't send me a call or a text.

"I will give that boy one more night. If he doesn't comply, I will have no choice but to send out an A.P.B on him. Give him a heads up. Maybe that will get his butt home."

"Alright."

After the message was sent, I went back to texting Arianna and filles her in on what was going on.

About two weeks passed and the A.P.B was sent out. He was nowhere to be found. Usually when he would run away, he would text me or call me. My mind couldn't help but go back to that horrid nightmare. Could it have been a premonition? I hoped to God that it wasn't the case.

Chapter Twenty-Two

Ares

To see Samora's health depreciate the way it did, only sickened me more. She showed up to school in sweatpants and rock t-shirts that were oversized and hid all of her curves. Just because I was pissed didn't mean that I didn't enjoy the view from time to time. She always had her hair straightened and in a sloppy bun now. The girl didn't even bother putting on makeup. If this was what she looked like when the guy was missing, I couldn't even imagine what she was going to look like after she found his body lying wrapped in plastic in her garage after school.

While I sat there making finger smudges through the condensation from my breath on the window, Someone slammed their heavy palms down on my shoulders. I turned around only to find stupid Erik behind me. He plopped down and frowned.

"Why do you always grimace at the sight of me?"

" I thought it was obvious that I didn't like you?"

"I would have thought you would have been sitting in the library with your precious Samora."

He made we cringe enough to gag. "You can have her. I'm not going to be anyone's rebound boy." The bell rang and I was over that conversation from the moment it began.

" A little birdy told me that you may have paid Juan a visit and sparked up another relationship with your Achilles heel."

I stopped in my tracks and put on the coolest expression that I could manage. "What?" I folded my arms. " Are you jealous that she is head over heels obsessed with me?"

He looked like he could strike at any moment. "I don't do leftovers." He shoved passed me on the way out. I couldn't help but smirk, knowing that I had him right where I wanted him and that was beneath my leather boot with him suffocating in a pile of feces.

When my last class of the day came to an end, I was stopped in the parking lot by Arianna. " What do you want?" I groaned.

"Samora is really suffering right now and a huge portion of it is because of you." She folded her arms.

" I highly doubt that. She can't let go of the past and that's why we are no longer even trying to be together."

"You sure do keep forgetting that you are in the same boat that you are. Would it kill you to just have a decent conversation with her like a human being. She will be heading straight home today and could use some acceptable closer." She marched off. After sitting in the student parking lot for like thirty minutes I decided that I really was dying to see her face when she saw his rotten corpse for the first time. Ooh just thinking about it was getting me turned on.

I drove out to her house and noticed that there was only one car in the driveway. I knew that things wouldn't be this freaking calm if she had already found him. Plus, it would be swarming with police and infested with yellow tape.

This was already starting to annoy me. I banged on her door with my fist. When she answered the door, she looked stunned. That was the most life I had seen in her in a while. Damn she was starting to appeal to my senses. Had to snap out of it.

" What are you doing here?" She swiped at a tear that escaped the corner of her left eye.

" Arianna said that you wanted to talk to me, but before I set foot in your house, I just want you to know that nothing will ever go back to the way things were. I'm over it."

"I know that you must hate me like crazy right now, but someone has come up missing and you're my only hope."

I cocked a brow. " What makes you think that I would do anything for you after all your bull?"

She tucked a stray hair behind her ear that had been bobbing in the wind. " Well, Erik told me that you were good at getting information about people."

I could have slammed his head through a brick wall. That was Erik's way of calling me a creepy stalker. He was just begging for me to put him in the damn grave. Instead, I gritted my teeth and composed a smile. " Who exactly are you trying to find?" She looked down at her feet and started twiddling her thumbs.

"Juan. I wouldn't have gotten involved if it were just at a friend's house, but he completely went off the radar."

Just before I could tell her it wasn't my problem, I heard the garage door start opening she dragged me into the house immediately by the arm. I knew that at any moment I would hear the sound of her father screaming his head off. To my astonishment, That never happened. How was this possible? Who he'll knew about me killing Juan? I snapped his neck. He didn't just walk away from the scene.

She shoved me into her closet and as I waited, I heard some shuffling and pages turning. I guess she was making it seem like she had been studying. Then I heard a light knock on her door and heavy footsteps along with the crunching noise of a paper bag.

"I thought it had been a while since the last time that I bought you take out."
She had better be sharing with me, I thought to myself. I deserved something out of this whacked out situation.

After he left, she got me out of the closet, and she offered me an egg roll.
I snatched it out of her hand. "Before you decline, please

just hear me out. If you do this, you might be saving someone's life tonight."

"What makes you think he died and doesn't just want to be bothered with you or his dad. I can't speak for him but as for myself, I hate it when girls get all chummy with my relatives. It's sort of disgusting."

" His father and I haven't always been on good terms. For him to call me and Juan not to respond to any of my messages, I just have this gut feeling that something terrible must have happened to him."

I needed some sort of excuse to scope out the garage, I didn't know how the heck I was going to pull it off, but I had to try. " Fine. Show me his email." She pulled it up on her phone. There was no pictures of another girl anywhere so I couldn't use that. He kept following this heavy metal band though. I bit down on my lower lip and checked for them being on tour. Sadly, they were going through drama and the lead singer was threatening to expose all their dirt if they didn't let him go solo. Apparently, there were some underaged girls from the high school and drugs that some speculated about on their site.

I pulled up his email address and hacked into his account. There were a few messages to one of his friends. The guy couldn't spell worth a crap, but he told this guy named Ryan that he was off to see Samora and he was really pumped up about it. That made me even more satisfied that the bastard was dead. I couldn't have the two of them going off in the sunset together. Unfortunately, Samora had been reading my phone screen over my shoulder.

" He was coming to meet me. Her brows pulled together. That doesn't make any sense as to why he didn't respond to me. I'm calling the police."

"Hold off on that." Spewed out of my mouth as I stole her phone from her. I could only imagine how shady I must have some off. Great! Now to come up with a convenient excuse.

" Why would I do that? He could be hurt, kidnapped or even dead!" Her eyes began to pool. Just watching her get so emotional over that pig made me want to kill her off too.

"You should text his friends and see if he may be with them." With that being said, she forwarded a message to everyone on his list. Long story short no one saw or heard from him. I had been in her bedroom for hours scoping out the territory.

Her windows had black and silver spirals on them, a desk made of glass in front of them. There were a few of her art pieces in black frames along the walls. She had a canopy bed with plush grey pillows along with a lavender and black comforter. The room. Her nightstands were mirror and there was a cute picture of her and her dad sitting on the beach. The bedroom Smelled like lavender just as I imagine it would smell like.

She tossed her phone on the bed and groaned after falling back into. Her pillows. I had to get the heck out of there before I did something, we both would regret.

"I promised my stepmom that I would be home an hour ago. " I scratched my head.

" Let me go see what part of the house my dad is in for the best exit strategy."

"Alright."

She came back and asked if it would be alright if I left through the garage.
Jack pot!

I felt sick to my stomach at the sight of a garage that only contained their boxed-up junk and her father's cheap ride. Someone had to have stolen the body which meant that I had been followed. But who!

Chapter Twenty-Three

Samora

Juan's father called the police and reported him missing. What happened next, was the most horrid thing I ever witnessed in my life. They found a decapitated body covered in plastic in a dumpster outside of a local bar in our town of all places. They later identified it as Juan, and I didn't know how to function. For him to be in our town that meant that someone killed him on his way to meet me. That also meant that he had to have been dead for him not to

respond to me. Months passed by and there was still no sign of the head anywhere. They had a closed casket funeral for him, and it was just too much heart ache for me to handle. I started skipping school adopted a smoking habit and ended up taking a GED while all my friends graduated and moved on with their lives.
Arianna and I still kept in touch and from time to time hung out, but the rest seemed to distance themselves that summer.

One afternoon when I finally mustered up enough courage to step outside the four corners of my house, I spotted a familiar car parked right outside the coffee shop that eventually became a haven for me when my dad started lecturing me about getting back into the thick of things again.

Ares stepped out of the car wearing a pair of designer shades and a black muscle shirt that had a silver skull on the front. His matching skinny jeans had slits in the knees and up the thighs. He looked even more handsome than he had before. It had been months since our last conversation and for some strange reason I was craving his attention. He lowered his glasses in my direction and strolled over.

"Wow! I'm speechless. How long has it been?" He slid out the chair in front of my table and took a seat.

"It's been a while." I forced a smile and tucked my hair behind my ears.

"Well, for what it's worth it's nice to see you again before I leave town." My heart sank to the pit of my stomach.

"Vacation?"

He slicked his hair back with his shades. " No. I got accepted to N.Y.C. I thought that it would be a great new start for me. I wouldn't have to ever see my dad and stepmother again."

Suddenly a whole crowd had gathered in front of the windows of the coffee shop. He and I joined the crowd and the cashier turned up the volume on the television. The last person's face that i ever thought to see again was plastered all over the screen.

"Oh my gosh!" I backed away from the window with my hand over my mouth and the other over my stomach."
He was in cuffs and forced into the back of a police car. He was found with Juan's severed head hurried in his backyard. That didn't make the least bit if sense. Erik may have been a jerk, but murder! Suddenly I started having all these flashbacks of when we were alone together, and it terrified the heck out of me.

What motive could Erik have possibly had for such a brutal murder? I knew that he slightly had a crush on me but how deep could those feelings have been? When I looked back on it, he seemed more like he was just playing games to get a rise out of Ares the entire time. This was some twisted crap.

"I don't believe this for a damn second. Erik might have been a real prick but him a killer?" Ares laughed.

"I don't know. This is too freaking out there for me."

" Who would bury a head of someone in their own backyard? This clearly must be a setup. I'm going to head down to the station and see what the heck is going on and what proof they had." He told me that he would call me back as soon as he got down to the bottom of it. I went home that night and cried myself to sleep.

When I went to sleep, I dreamt of being in a graveyard. I got down on my knees in front of Juan's tombstone. Then I fell back at the sight of leather boots planted on top of it. Juan had his head in his hand and suddenly bats the size of whales swooped down and carried him off leaving behind his head which dropped in my lap. I screamed my head off and sprang to my feet. " Samora!" My father's voice came out of Juan's mouth and the world around me began to quake. The next thing I knew, I was literally screaming my head off into my dad's chest.

"It was just a nightmare." He rocked me back and forth. Tears started rolling and I felt like the wind had been knocked out of me and someone was slicing my heart open with a thousand tiny razor blades. How much more could I take? Was it not enough to find him dead? Were things ever going to get back to normal again for me?

Arianna came over as soon as she heard the news. She was just about as shocked as Ares and most likely the entire student body.

"Ares still hasn't messaged or called me back. We should go down to the station to see what's up." That was when my father came back in.

"You aren't going anywhere near that police station. They won't let you back there to see him now, even if you wanted to. Besides, he was convicted of murder."

Once again, I ended up feeling useless while there was a huge problem that desperately needed to be solved. Thongs got so bad emotionally for me that the only place my dad permitted me to go to be a Councilor, who got me on anxiety and depression medication.

I sat there in her office after about twenty minutes of silence. The woman was obsessed with sunshine and dolphins because if there wasn't a painting there was a sculpture or Knick- knack. Her name was Mrs. Rhinestone.

She was petite with salt and pepper strands of hair on her head. She had wrinkles in the center of her forehead and bags beneath her eyes. She was very pale and very patient with me after all he'll I'd given her.

"I saw that a friend of yours was arrested today on the news. Surely you must have something to say about it. I would hate to go another quiet session with you again."

Chapter Twenty- Three

Section Ares

After being kicked out of the station, my phone went off. When it did Megan's number was displayed on the screen. When I didn't answer, she sent me a text message that made my heart stop for a second. I quickly calls het psycho behind up.

" Megan! Where the heck are you?" My blood was pumping hard and fast.

"Now, is that anyway to reply to the person who saved your ass?" I could have strangled her for sounding so freaking calm about it.

"How stupid do you think I am? I wouldn't want to end up like Dion on your dear old mommy."

I hopped into the car and started gunning the gas like a mad man down the street.

"Why did you do this?"

"Isn't it obvious? This ensures that you will be with me forever and stop hanging around that tramp any more. She hurt and used you. For that she has to pay for it. I saw the way she was attached to Erik when you weren't around. She would have toyed with you guys until you killed yourselves off. Don't worry I'm fixing everything. Pretty soon she will be out of your hair too. Once the police find out about the secret text messages that she sent to him both her and Erik will be locked up for good and we can start working on our future together."

I never thought this bitch had it in her to do something so diabolical. This was the first time that I saw her as my equal. That wasn't something I ever anticipated. However, since she was bat shit crazy like I was then that meant that I would have to eliminate her before all my plans went up in smoke. There was absolutely nothing sexy about a female being my level of crazy. She was a freaking loose cannon and there was no way in hell I was going to be sleeping with one eye open at night, waiting for her to turn against me.

I camped out in the alley and scoped out her house to see if her bedroom light might have been on. Every window in the house was blacked out, so I hauled ass down the road until I reached Samara's house. Her bedroom light was on. I spotted her changing into her silky pink pajamas. Before the light went out. I got out of the car and walked around the perimeter to make sure that little Ms. Psycho wasn't in the venue.

I literally camped out there until the crack of dawn to make sure Megan didn't get her. To be thorough, I followed Samora into town. She was headed to the grocery store with her dad. I kept hidden at a distance the entire time and made sure that they got home safe.

Then Megan called again. "At this rate you might as well move in with her."

"You've been stalking me!"

"Why don't you just stop trying to hinder me from making our lives better? I officially apologies to you for everything that I did wrong. You will trust me again. I promise." She hung up before I could get another word in.

I called up Samora and told her to let me in. A few minutes later she opened the gate. I couldn't help but look around for any hidden spots that the crazy chick could have been before following her inside and getting my things.

Samora cocked a brow at me. "Don't get too excited sweetheart. I'm just doing this as a safety precaution."

"Have you lost your mind! My dad won't let you stay in my room."

"Which is why you aren't going to tell him. I will explain everything once we are in the safety of your bedroom."

She hesitated before the door. "Oh, come on already." I opened the door myself. Once that was said and done, I dropped my bag at the foot of her bed and took out my sleeping bag and pillow. Once I was settled in, she took my bag and placed it in her closet.

" This is going to be where you hide if my dad comes strolling in. Got it?"
I rolled my eyes. She took a seat on her bed with her arms folded. " Care to tell me why the heck you and I are having a sleepover?"

I didn't exactly want to throw any names into the pot of suspicion at the moment. I couldn't have Samora getting Megan thrown behind bars because the bitch would take me down with her. I might have ended up needing to eliminate her.

"There's no freaking way that Erik is responsible for the murder of your ex. Until the police get this thing sorted out, I don't want you to be unprotected. The killer might know where you live for all I know."

She folded her arms. "I thought that you were leaving to New York?"

"Plans can change." I shrugged. "I don't know about you but I'm starving." That kept her occupied instead of interacting me all afternoon. When she came back upstairs, she placed a plate with a sandwich in my lap. I lifted the top piece of bread and discovered that it was a turkey sandwich with lettuce tomato, cheese and she was even kind enough to put my favorite mayo on it.

"I hope that it's not too cheap for your expensive pallet." I took a huge chunk out of it and gave her a thumbs up.

I laid there on my sleeping bag searching through the internet about any other details that they may have had on Erik's case while she did homework. It was so frustrating because there was nothing that I didn't already know.

I felt eyes on me and met Samora's gaze. She gulped then guarded her eyes as she asked if I found anything. " Sadly, no." I took a stretch.

"I know that he is capable of doing some messed up garbage, but murder seems a bit much."

I laughed. "No kidding. Didn't we already cover this?" When Dion was alive, he mainly kept him around to cover us whenever we. Did our dirt or needed some equipment for whatever the heck that we planned for the day. The real threat was laying only a few centimeters away from her and she didn't even have a clue.

"How do you think I feel about it. I am not shooting rainbows out if my butt and hopping on clouds right now." She was intrigued and started scribbling away on her notepad.

"Do you think that he could be capable of something like that?"

I uncrossed my legs and scooted to the edge of my seat. "I wasn't even aware that they knew each other existed until today." I started gnawing the inside of my cheek, wondering what she possibly could be writing down on that stupid note pad of hers.

When I stepped outside of that therapy session, I hated to admit it, but I surprised myself when I really opened up to her about my thoughts. A small portion of weight felt as if it had been lifted from my shoulders.

Chapter Twenty- Three

Section:

- Samora-

I woke up to the sound of Ares snoring like a pig and his phone blasting heavy metal. I quickly snatched his phone from his chest before my father could barge in and complain. I turned the ringer off and rolled my eyes at the sight of Megan's name displayed on the screen.

When I didn't answer, it vibrated, and I debated with myself about whether or not I was going to take a peek at his notification tab. My thumb was one step ahead of me and I started reading right away.

Megan: You really need to stop being so uptight. Once they find out that Erik's innocent then they will have no choice but to set him free. It will be a cold case. Please call me back as soon as you get the chance.

That set off a thousand of unanswered questions in my mind. She couldn't have killed Juan because she didn't know who he was. There was no motive whatsoever. So, strange. I quickly placed his phone back over his stomach and pretended to be asleep as he woke up a few minutes later.

He removed a strand of hair from my face and tucked it ever so gently behind my ear. Then let out a sigh. "You poor thing. You haven't the slightest idea about what I have to deal with." Then I heard him get up and open the window and once he was out of sight, I sat up took a stretch and grabbed my clothes after a hot shower, I cleaned up his things before my dad knocked on the door.
"I will be getting home late tonight. I left some cash on the counter. Order whatever you like."

As I shut my closet, I told him thanks.

"Alrighty then. Have a good day and stay out of trouble."

"Okay. Have a good day at work."

I grabbed the cash off the table and headed over to the coffee shop. There I ran into Erik of all people. I was so excited to see him, I gave him a hug without thinking the situation completely through. When I pulled away from him, we were both blushing.

I cleared my throat and looked down at the floor as I spoke. " I'm shocked that you didn't greet me with a pitchfork and chainsaw." He laughed.

"Well, I know that you had nothing to do with Juan's murder. I am curious about why someone would put his remains in your backyard though. Is there anyone that might be a mutual enemy to both you and Juan?"

He scratched the top of his head. " I have a ton of enemies, but None that I can think of that would tie me to your ex." I couldn't help but frown. He placed a hand on my shoulder. " Hey, things will turn around. Why don't we grab a table together for old time's sake."

I ordered an iced coffee, and he ordered a regular with no creamer. I always took him for the extra sugar type. But I once thought that Juan and I were going to get married.

Once we were seated, I placed my drink on a napkin before taking a sip. " This is really nice to have a coffee with you before I leave town."

I gasped. " Where are you going?"

"In case you haven't noticed, there is someone who killed a guy and is trying to blame me for it." He laughed. " It didn't exactly go over too well with the dean at the college of my dreams, so it's high time that I ditch this town and not look back. It was great to finally get to know you after all these years. I wish we could have met sooner, and you actually got to know the real me." He sighed.

" Well, for what it was worth, I hope that you find some cool new people and have a better experience than you did here."

He pursed his lips together and gave mean nod. After that we said an official goodbye to one another, and I returned home for the night.

Chapter Twenty-Three

Section

-Ares-

Megan agreed to meet me at the abandoned train station on the out skirts of town. Tonight, would be the night that I set things straight before the psychopath hurt anyone else.

The moon hug high in the sky and there were a few stars. The wind was warm. I kicked around a rock or two as I waited for her to show up. She was dressed in black leather pants a grey frilly blouse and a smirk that I would have liked to smack off her face.

She stopped three paces in front of me. " I hate the way you look at me now. You. Being under appreciated was always something that you and I struggled with. You would think that you would show some gratitude after I cleaned up your mess the other day." She frowned.

" You had no business meddling in my affairs."

"Would it have made you happy to rot behind bars? I can arrange that for you with just one phone call. " She pulled her phone from her back pocket and started dialing. I snatched the phone from her and shut it off, before returning it to her. " That's what I thought."

" What will it take for all of this to go away?"

She placed a hand on my cheek. I stepped back. " I want you to be with me forever. It's as simple as that."

" That's never going to happen. You know this."

She started laughing like a hyena, scaring me half to death. " I figured that you would say that, so to make sure that I got what I wanted, she handed over a tape recorder that had a blue sticky note on it that read play me in green sharpie.

I cocked a brow at her. " Seriously? Who the heck carries these anymore?"

She rolled her eyes. "Just listen to it already!"

I pressed play.at first there was some static then I heard the sound of a door opening. " Hello Megan." My father said in a surprised voice. " I don't think Ares is around."

" I'm actually here to check on you. You must have had a rough recovery." Then there was a sound of footsteps and then the door closed.

"That was awfully thoughtful of you to check on me like this."

"Why wouldn't I? You're like the father I always wanted." Then there was a loud tweak, and the recording went back to static.

My blood was boiling I crushed the tiny tape recorder with my bare hands and chucked it at the skank. Its pieces grazed her cheek. It gave me enough time to snag her by the hair. " Where the heck so he?" She started laughing again. "Not until you submit to me and give up that slut."

"You have some nerve screwing with a murderer right now. I can easily add you to the body count." I said through clenched teeth as she attempted to resist.

" You think I came alone?" Suddenly. Something hard broke across my back. I heard my own bones snap upon impact. I dropped to the jacked-up platform, taking her down with me.

She squirmed to her feet. I snagged her by the ankle before being hit again. Then her left boot slammed into my side rib repeatedly. I spat blood in her face after the big guy wearing a black hoodie and skull mask turned me over. He reached into his hoodie and pulled out a white napkin before it was lights out for me.

When I woke up, I found myself chained to a pole in some sort of basement. The walls contained old movie posters and ratted out tan and brown furniture. I could hear a few mice scurrying about. It was dimly lit and smelled of black mold which seemed to coat the walls like algae.

I jumped at the sound of coughing nearby. It seemed to be coming from above the basement. Then the old splintered up door opened.

"Wow! I'm impressed by how much of me rubbed off on you." She smirked at me. "Just out of curiosity, where's my father?"

" All in good time." She stopped in front of me and pulled out her phone. "Bring her in." She said in an emotionless tone of voice.

The next thing I knew masked boy came in with unconscious Samora over his shoulder. The fury within ignited like a surging fire about to torch anyone who came into contact with me. In spite of the stupid ropes, I still strained and squirmed to get free.

" But first, I thought that I would put an end to roadblock number one. Why you wasted your precious time trying to get into her pants is beyond me. She gives off those virgin vibes." She had her accomplice place her on the floor in front of me. Then he reached into his pocket and handed over a box cutter to Megan. With a crooked smile she removed Samora's hair out of her face and gently ran the blade a few centimeters over the flesh of Samora's neck. My heart was beating faster than a hamster on a treadmill. She watched my reaction with satisfaction.

"Don't worry." She got back into standing position. " I'm not selfish." She walked over to me and swayed the blade from side to side in my face slowly. " I will set your father free, but however there is a tiny price you must pay to set him free." She snickered.

" You must add her to your precious collection."

Why the heck was I not surprised?

I already had that on my to do list. She chose Juan over me and I thought that I would put the loser out of her misery so, I didn't have to deal with her anymore. This, However was far from what I had in mind. I wanted to get laid first in a place of my choosing. But that didn't stop me from playing along. I could at least set the stage of conquering hero.

"You must be out of your mind." I sat in her face." She wiped it with a scowl.

" I figured that you still wanted to be with this trash. It must suck knowing that she will never utterly understand you like I do, or love you like I do. I will take you flaws and all. They are a huge turn on for me. You don't have to pretend to be something you aren't."

"I have never been attracted to myself, so I think you have been disqualified from my bang list."

She back handed me across the face before quickly running that box cutter across my mid-thigh. The sting of open flesh when damp air hit it was exhilarating and painful. She grabbed my face and kissed me before giving me gentle slap to the face. "I am all about second chances. Your naughty boy. "She bit down on her bottom lip and told me that for my punishment I would stay without food or water until she returned. That could have been hours from then. She strung up Samora to a chair that skull man brought down after her visit. He strategically placed her a few feet in front of me.

This was all going according to plan. Megan was a creature of habit still. I found out long ago how to handle her. She had a case of bipolar disorder. Once I caught onto it before she and I split, I took full advantage of it. I could piss her off then the next day she would greet me with arms wide open like nothing ever happened. She hated being medicated because it made her feel powerless, and I knew that she hadn't changed a bit in that department.

The following day, Skull face returned and doped Samora up with another batch of chloroform. "Let me guess, you're the silent but deadly type?" I was disappointed that he didn't give me a comeback or punch in the face. He just grunted and disappeared upstairs.

I usually took my morning pee, but I would rather contract a UTI or a bladder infection before I pissed myself. That didn't stop me from squirming around here and there. My bladder literally felt like it might explode at any point in time. This was the most uncomfortable situation that I had ever found myself in. A long time ago I used to be into that tying people up thing. After this experience, I was far from aroused. It was also boring as hell. My stomach even started rumbling and my body was growing numb.

Thankfully, Megan graced me with her presence accompanied by skull face, who brought in my dad. However, unlike Samora he was sporting a black eye, busted lip and a battered torso. Seeing him like this was enough to set anyone off. "After seeing what my friend is capable of, I think that our paths have aligned." Skull guy handed her the box cutter. She strolled over to me and looked me directly in the eye as. Mine blazed with wrath. I already compiled thousands of unholy ways to murder her, and I couldn't wait to use one. "You've seen what my friend can do if you double cross me." She slit through the ropes with the box cutter. I dropped to my knees feeling exhausted and feeling tingly life come back slowly to my legs.

"You really are one psycho bitch." I laughed.

"That's why you love me." She leant me her shoulder to walk me over to Samora. Just an appraiser. I told myself. I plotted this moment for an exceptionally long time during my uncomfortable stay at the chamber of hell.

She handed over the box cutter. The skull guy was standing right behind Samora with her neck exposed and a clump of her hair in his fist. "I don't know why you want her unconscious through all of this. Wouldn't it have been more satisfying to have the victim conscious?"

"Maybe you should stop talking, or I might have you join her."

Promises, promises.

I made a quick slit in her neck but not deep enough to cause harm. I had Dion to thank for that. Then quickly spun around to face Megan before she knew what hit her and with a little extra force her hand flew up to her blood spurting neck before hitting to ground.

Skull man frog leaped over Samora and knocked me to the ground. He started slamming down on my back like nobody's business. While he was beating me to a pulp, my shake hand extended out towards the box cutter a few centimeters away. Bones were breaking beneath those iron fists of his. Blood was spilling out of my mouth. This was life or death and I sure as hell wasn't about to die here. I channeled what bit of rage and energy I had left and focused it on the prize. He captured the blade before I could get a finger on it. Then jerked my head up with a hand full of my hair and was about to go for the kill when I heard a thwack! And big boy came toppling down on the side of me. My father had regained consciousness and knocked the jack ads out cold with a broken piece of wood from the rubble. He had more strength than I did and was in the worst condition.

After extensive investigation and wasted time. I was freed from jail under the charges man slaughter. Several years later.

Chapter Twenty- three

Section
- Samora-

I found myself lying in a hospital room with the faint sound of snoring that came from my father, who had his head on the side of my bed. Along with the sound of a beeping heart monitor. I shuttered from how cold it was in the room. My dad jerked awake. Then he quickly rose and embraced me. The last thing that I remembered before it was lights out was parting ways with Erik.

Later on, that afternoon, Ares dropped in and told me everything. I just couldn't believe that Megan would go through such great lengths to keep him. From what I had seen, you would have thought she didn't care as much. I knew that it would take a crap ton of therapy for me to ever even grasp just an inch of sanity back to my life again.

Several years later...

I had just got off the plane and was heading straight over to the baggage claim area to retrieve my suite case when I accidentally bumped into someone that I hadn't seen in years. Ares. He took a. Step back. Both of us shocked and embarrassed. His hair was shoulder length and behind his ears. My heart started pounding like crazy when he gave me a crooked smile and removed his sunglasses.

"You are back for vacation too?"

"Just for two days." His eyes were too intense for me to look into, so I guarded them by looking down at his feet. He reached into my pocket and placed his number in my phone. " it was nice to see you." He handed me the phone before he left.

He reached into my pocket and placed his number in my phone. " it was nice to see you." He handed me the phone before he left.